REASONS TO BE PROUD TO BE SCOTTISH

RICHARD HAPPER

MAGICAL MOMENTS IN SCOTLAND'S HISTORY

PORTICO

First published in the United Kingdom in 2013 by
Portico
1 Gower Street
London
WC1E 6HD

An imprint of Pavilion Books Company Ltd

ISBN 9781907554872

A CIP catalogue record for this book is available from the British Library.

10 9 8 7 6 5 4 3 2

Printed and bound by 1010 Printing Ltd, China

This book can be ordered direct from the publisher at www.pavilionbooks.com

We look to Scotland for all our ideas of civilization.

VOLTAIRE

INTRODUCTION

You probably know that Scotland has a very proud history of inventors, discoverers, explorers, artists and all-round braw folk.

Every day, in every corner of the world, people enjoy a proud Scottish achievement: they watch television, talk on the phone, sip a whisky, play a round of golf, take penicillin, and pay for it all by going to the cash machine.

But there are even more reasons to be proud of our brilliant wee country than you might think.

Did you know that Scots invented the blackboard? The detective agency? The lawnmower? The bicycle? Radar? And the golden retriever? Bet you never knew that.

Economics, geology, sociology, oceanography – Scots pioneered those entire disciplines. Hospitals would still ring to screams of agony and thousands would be felled by ordinary bugs if it weren't for our magnificent medical advances. New York and Tokyo would look very different without lights filled with neon (yes, discovered by a Scot).

INTRODUCTION

Cannons forged in Falkirk helped Britannia rule the waves. Scots founded the Territorial Army, the first sniper unit, the RAF and the SAS. London's docks and bridges, England's canals and railways, Japan's ships and mines – Scottish expertise built them all.

Our actors are the toast of Hollywood, our musicians have rocked the world, children grow up reading our classic stories: *Peter Pan*, *The Wind in the Willows*, *Treasure Island.* A Scotsman even voiced Mickey Mouse!

We made the first smooth roads and the tyres that roll upon them, the waterproof coat and the welly boot (no great surprise given our weather).

We are world-beaters – you can watch a film in the world's tallest cinema, soak up culture at the world's largest arts festival and admire the world's tallest hedge.

And how the hell could you handle a hangover without a can of IRN-BRU?

So pour yourself a dram, get out some oatcakes or maybe a caramel wafer, pull a tartan rug over your knees and enjoy *365 Reasons To Be Proud To Be Scottish*!

Richard Happer

SCOTTISH GLOSSARY

AIYAH	Ouch
BAMPOT	Idiot
BUNNET	Flat hat, bonnet
CARKS IT	To die
CLARTY	Dirty
DREICH	A bit rainy, a bit misty, a bit grey. Scotland's weather, basically
LOUPING	Leaping
MIDDEN	Literally, a rubbish tip, a mess
OUTWITH	Beyond, outside
PISH	Really not very good at all. Piss
POLIS	Police
SHOOGLIEST	Most shoogly. That which jiggles around in an unstable way
STOOSHIE	Uproar, an enjoyable fight
TAMMY	A flat hat with a bobble, usually of the tartan persuasion

JANUARY

HOT-SHOT SCOT

James Braidwood was an apprentice surveyor from Edinburgh who wasn't that interested in constructing things; his burning passion was how fire destroyed buildings. In 1824 he founded the world's first municipal fire service in Edinburgh and later published the first fire-fighters' manual. He became director of the fledgling London Fire Brigade today in 1833 and it's pretty much thanks to him that the modern fire service, as we know it, exists. Which means, ladies, that next time you are dreaming of a man in firefighting uniform rescuing a stranded cat down from a tree, spare a quick thought of thanks for James Braidwood, the man who is credited with creating the uniforms and, by doing so, lighted the flame of a billion female fantasies around the world!

GIN
TONIC

JUST THE TONIC

Ah, can anything beat a long, cool G&T at the end of the day? It's delicious, relaxing and a pretty good cure for malaria. George Cleghorn from Granton was a brilliant young doctor who today in 1736 was appointed an army surgeon in Minorca. After years of research on the frequent diseases that ravaged the island, he published a treatise showing *how* quinine bark – known for some years to be an effective remedy – acted as a cure for malaria. It was the first effective treatment of the disease. Quinine, of course, is also the flavour in tonic water.

THE ELECTRIC VILLAGE THAT TURNED TO ICE

The grand honour of being the first village in the world to have every house connected to electricity belongs to Kinlochleven in the Highlands. This was thanks to the hydroelectric scheme built in 1907 to power the local aluminium smelter. When this closed the site was reborn today in 2004 as another world-beater – the biggest indoor ice-climbing wall on the planet. And there's a lovely micro-brewery there, too.

LET'S GET STEAMING

Transport history was made today in 1803 with the successful demonstration of the *Charlotte Dundas*, the world's first practical steamboat. The venue was the Forth and Clyde Canal, which in those days wasn't full of Tesco trolleys. Within months the boat was towing pairs of 70-ton barges all the way to Glasgow at the heady speed of 2mph, proving that steam power was here to stay and outpacing the average Scotrail train.

WATT A GENIUS

James Watt was a humble lab technician at Glasgow University when he was given a model of Newcomen's rudimentary steam engine and told to fix it. Watt did, and realised how inefficient it was. Then, while walking on Glasgow Green one Sunday, he suddenly realised how he could make it better – with a condenser. This revolutionary idea kept hot and cold steam separate, and Watt's new steam engine (patented today in 1769) would literally power the Industrial Revolution.

CHALK UP ANOTHER FIRST FOR SCOTLAND

A simple Scottish invention has probably given the world more ingenious ideas than any other in history: the blackboard. There isn't a classroom or lecture hall in the world that hasn't had one, but the very first was put up by James Pillans, headmaster of the Royal High School in Edinburgh, today in 1801. He also came up with the idea of using different-coloured chalks (actually gypsum), which he used to teach geography. Presumably he was also the first to lob a blackboard duster at a pupil's head.

THE EXTRA WHO DESERVES A STARRING ROLE

Thomas Edison is usually held to be the inventor of motion-picture production. But many of his most important breakthroughs were actually made by Scotsman William Dickson, who worked for his company. Dickson not only built an early motion-picture camera, he also perfected the standard 35mm film, which he patented today in 1894.

THE REALLY GOOD BOOK

The most famous book in English was commissioned by a Scotsman, King James VI of Scotland and I of England, today in 1604 when he authorised a translation of the Bible. The result is recognised as a literary masterpiece that remains the most influential version of the most influential book in the world. It is also the most common source of phrases in English, beating even Shakespeare, giving hundreds of expressions to the language, including 'sign of the times', 'in the twinkling of an eye', 'land of Nod' and 'eat, drink and be merry'.

SILLY GHILLIES

The ghillie suit is a form of camouflage where you basically attach half the contents of a forest to your clothing. Scottish gamekeepers created it partly to help them sneak up on their prey more easily, and also because it was simply great fun. The Lovat Scouts, a Scottish Highland regiment formed today in 1900, were the first military unit to use ghillie suits. Affectionately described as 'half wolf and half jackrabbit', they went on to become the British Army's first ever sniper unit in the First World War.

NOT QUITE THE REAL MCCOY

Strangely enough, the phrase 'the real McCoy' is not even the real McCoy itself! It was coined by Messrs Mackay of Edinburgh, who made a brand of fine whisky from 1856 onwards that they promoted as 'A drappie o' the real MacKay'. The phrase was quoted by Robert Louis Stevenson, but was later corrupted to 'the real McCoy' in a Canadian novel, *The Rise and Fall of the 'Union Club'*, published today in 1881.

MAGIC MOVE

J.K. Rowling originally hails from Gloucestershire, but it was in Scotland that the young wizard Harry Potter first came to life. Rowling moved to Edinburgh with her young daughter in 1993 and wrote her first books in the warmth of the city's coffee shops, particularly the Elephant House (which, in true thrifty Scots fashion, now does a profitable line in Potter-themed coffee). By the time she finished the last book today in 2007 she had graduated from cafés to five-star hotels, famously writing a celebratory message on a marble bust in her room at the Balmoral.

RUNAWAY BRIDE - AND GROOM

With 5,000 weddings a year, Gretna Green is one of the world's most popular nuptial destinations. It's thanks to the Marriage Act of 1753 (First Reading on this day), which tightened wedding requirements in England but not Scotland. Here, lads aged fourteen and lasses of just twelve could marry without parental consent and the ceremony needed only two witnesses. As the first building in the first village over the border, this turned the blacksmith's shop at Gretna into the eighteenth century equivalent of those Elvis Presley chapels you see all over Las Vegas.

WHERE'S EVERYBODY ELSE?

You'd think by now we'd have learned not to mess around in Afghanistan. Back in the first Anglo–Afghan war, British forces had captured Kabul but were then forced out by an Afghan uprising. A convoy of 4,500 troops and 12,000 camp followers set out for Jalalabad. The Afghans had other ideas, and the only member of the entire army to reach safety (today in 1842) was William Brydon of Ross-shire – an assistant surgeon and one tough Scotsman – who rode into Jalalabad with half his skull missing to an Afghan sword. A few dozen captives were later released, but most of the 16,500 who set out were killed.

NAIRN WIPES FLOOR WITH RIVALS

When Michael Nairn decided to get into the booming floorcloth business he borrowed £4,000 today in 1847 to build his first factory in Kirkcaldy. Profits were slow coming: the cloth was at that time dried by the heat of the sun, which – this being Scotland – took bloody ages! Locals dubbed his factory in Nether Street 'Nairn's Folly'. But by 1877, Kirkcaldy was the world's largest producer of linoleum, with six manufacturers in the town. Nairn's company is still there today, the world's oldest and largest linoleum maker, helping to give the town its unique aroma.

TA, MAC!

Next time you're stuck in a tailback on the M8, don't despair – enjoy your chance to consider the wondrous Scottishness of the road surface that you are standing stationary upon. Before Ayrshire-born John Loudon McAdam paved the way, roads were usually rutted or muddy nightmares. Taking the job of Surveyor-General for roads around Bristol today in 1816, his big idea was to build the surface up using layers of different-sized stones. By the end of the nineteenth century, 90 per cent of European roads were 'macadamised', allowing traffic to zip along far faster than before. Or not, as the case may be.

DOCTOR, NO!

Not many people have been one of the twentieth century's most influential psychotherapists *and* a maverick icon of counter-culture. R.D. Laing from Govanhill shot to rock-star-level fame in the 1960s when he denounced normality for being mad and radically challenged contemporary psychology. His classic book *The Divided Self* (published today in 1960) argued that psychosis comes from tension between two personas within us: our authentic, private identity, and the false, 'sane' self we present to the world. It wasn't all dusty theory with Laing, either – he also apparently had LSD and whisky sessions with Sean Connery.

A CORNY STORY

Ever made your runny gravy thick and delicious with cornflour? You and your roast chicken have John Polson of Paisley to thank. Polson experimented with the starches in his dad's muslin factory and eventually worked out how to remove the fat from maize and so create an edible starch. He patented this today in 1854 and marketed it as 'Brown and Polson's Patent Corn Flour'. As well as salvaging Sunday dinners, cornflour is a vital ingredient in custards, baby food and blancmange.

ICE IDEA

Cold beers, chilled milk, ice cream, frozen peas – you enjoy them all thanks to William Cullen from Hamilton. Cullen was a brilliant chemist and physician who today in 1756 created artificial refrigeration for the first time. He used a pump to create a vacuum over a container of diethyl ether, which absorbed heat from the surrounding air, forming ice. Pretty nifty, but Cullen was more interested in ideas than commerce, so the world had to wait 200 more years for Cornettos.

SHE BANGS THE DRUMS

Evelyn Glennie from Aberdeenshire is a virtuoso percussionist (and the first full-time solo percussionist) in twentieth century Western society – despite being profoundly deaf. She regularly plays barefoot during live performances and studio recordings in order to feel the music better. It also looks pretty cool. She has played with dozens of leading orchestras, and recorded with some of music's biggest names. But she really hit the big time today in 2001 when she appeared on *Sesame Street*, playing Oscar the Grouch's trashcans.

THE SHAPE OF DRINKS TO COME

Next time you uncork a nice bottle of red, raise your glass to Leith. For it was here, in the glassworks on Baltic Street (founded today in 1746), that the classic wine-bottle shape was designed. The glassworks produced up to 1 million of the parallel-sided, round-shouldered, narrow-neck bottles every week, and the pattern became the plonk-producers' standard.

SWEET DREAMS COME TRUE

Eurythmics had been kicking around the music scene in one form or another for years without much luck. But with the US release of their second album *Sweet Dreams* today in 1983 they really hit the big time. The title track became a dance classic and the duo enjoyed a string of worldwide chart successes. Aberdeen-born lead singer Annie Lennox quickly became a pop icon and one of the most successful female artists in music history.

JANUARY

THE PEOPLE'S PUSSY

22

The People's Palace and Winter Gardens in Glasgow (opened today in 1898) was one of the first museums in the world to focus on the lives of ordinary people, rather than on artefacts pinched by toffs on their holidays. It is also famous for having the first cat ever to join a trade union. Smudge, employed in 1979 to handle an outbreak of vermin, made the headlines in the 1980s when she got her card for the General, Municipal and Boilermakers trade union as a 'blue collar' worker.

STEWART SHOOTS TO NO. 1

Proud Scots will go to almost any lengths to be the best or the first. But James Stewart, Earl of Moray, claimed an unintentional – and unwelcome – first today in 1570. He was the half-brother of Mary Queen of Scots but he disapproved of her marriage to Lord Darnley. After several years of court intrigues and military skirmishes he was shot and killed on this day by one of Mary's supporters. It was the first *ever* recorded assassination by a firearm. Well done, Jamie!

ADAM'S SENSE OF STYLE

If your dad's a genius it can be a bit tricky choosing the same career. Robert Adam's pa was superstar architect William Adam, but the lad was certainly ambitious and today in 1755 he arrived in Italy in search of the skills and experience that would help him surpass his father's achievements. With his brothers, Robert became a pioneer of the classical revival that would hugely influence the development of Western architecture, both in Europe and in North America.

POETIC PISS-UP

Burns Night started out as an annual supper held in Ayrshire by friends of the famous poet on the anniversary of his death. It now marks his birthday (today in 1759), with thousands of people spending the evening reading poems, drinking whisky, and boiling and stabbing perfectly innocent haggii. After Queen Victoria and Columbus, Robert Burns has more statues dedicated to him around the world than any other non-religious figure.

I DESIRE THEREFORE I AM

David Hume was a genius philosopher and all-round brainbox who went to Edinburgh University aged ten. A brilliant writer, Hume pioneered the essay as a literary genre and started his first major work, *A Treatise of Human Nature*, aged sixteen. It was published over ten years later, today in 1739, and is now considered one of the greatest philosophical works ever written. He proposed that desire, not reason, governs human behaviour. You might think that it wouldn't take a genius to work that one out...

FIFE FLIES THE FLAG

Naval captain John Strong was the first to land on some new-found islands in the South Atlantic today in 1690. He promptly named them the Falklands after the owner of his ship, Viscount Falkland, who in turn was named after Falkland Palace in Fife. We can also be proud of the palace itself, which has the world's oldest tennis court still in use, built in 1539.

TRANSVESTITE TUESDAY

Shetland's 'Up Helly Aa' is Europe's largest fire festival and one of the world's great parties. It marks the end of the Yule season and features parades of 'guizers' in fancy dress (pissed-up blokes in drag, basically), a torch-lit procession and the burning of a full-size replica Viking galley. There is then a long, long night of dancing and drinking in halls throughout Lerwick. Traditionally held on the last Tuesday in January, if you fancy attending then 2014's jollies will be on this day. The following day is a local holiday, simply because everyone is far too bladdered to do any work whatsoever.

SMYTH TAKES A CLOSER LOOK

Charles Piazzi Smyth was a man whose achievements are worth remembering. Appointed Astronomer Royal in Scotland today in 1846, he pioneered the idea that telescopes are best placed high up to avoid atmospheric disturbance. Later he became the first man to photograph the interior of the Great Pyramid of Giza. But the best thing about Smyth was his sheer brass neck: realising that Scottish weather conditions were, shall we say, less than ideal for star-watching, he promptly demanded the Admiralty relocate his office to Tenerife. Amazingly, they agreed. Maybe we should all try that...

DAVY DOES JUST DANDY

An Arbroath lad called David Dunbar emigrated from Scotland to live in America and worked in a plumbing company before trying his luck as inventor. His method for enamelling iron baths is still in use, but his overhead valve engine was his breakout success. Virtually all modern engines are derivatives of this innovation. He founded his own motor company today in 1904, which became the country's largest car-maker and is now the oldest active American make. Dunbar was David's middle name – his surname was Buick.

HE FELT THE EARTH MOVE

31

Blacksmith's son James Porteous left Haddington aged twenty-five and settled in California, where he found some success making wagons. But he really hit pay dirt with his 'Fresno Scraper' (patented today in 1889), which could lift and move soil four times faster than a man with a spade. The Fresno Scraper transformed land levelling, ditch digging and road building. One of the most important engineering machines ever made, it was vital to the building of the Panama Canal and formed the basis of the modern bulldozer. Porteous shifted loads of them.

FEBRUARY

LET THERE BE LIGHTHOUSE

By the turn of the eighteenth century, the Bell Rock in the North Sea was wrecking at least six ships every winter. So engineer Robert Stevenson designed the tallest offshore lighthouse in the world. Standing 115ft high, it was first lit today in 1811 and is visible from 35 miles away. The challenges of building the lighthouse on a barely visible rock 11 miles off the coast of Angus made it one of the Seven Wonders of the Industrial World. It is now the world's oldest surviving sea-washed lighthouse and was constructed so brilliantly that the masonry has not been replaced or adapted in 200 years.

'THE GREAT MONTROSE'

James Graham, Marquess of Montrose, was a near-mythic seventeenth century general who united some frankly rabble-like Highland clans into a formidable fighting force. He may have changed sides a couple of times, but Montrose produced one of the most remarkable hot streaks in military history. With daring and discipline his armies crushed their opponents in six battles in a row, including at Inverlochy today in 1645. He was later hanged for being a traitor and had his head stuck on a spike, but for a while there he was very much the man to beat.

FORTH FERRY IS FIRST

The world's first ferry to carry a passenger train began today in 1850 across the Forth. Trains rolled on to a boat called the *Leviathan* at Granton then sailed five miles over the Firth of Forth to Burntisland where they rolled off onto tracks heading north. The ferry operated successfully for 40 years until the railway company built the equally historic Forth Bridge in 1890.

COCKSURE COCHRANE

You're doing all right when the French nickname you *Le Loup des Mers* ('The Sea Wolf'). Admiral Thomas Cochrane from Lanarkshire was a daring and successful captain of the Napoleonic Wars who later led the rebel navies of Chile, Brazil and Greece. Today in 1820 he captured Valdivia, then the most fortified place in South America, with just 300 men and two ships. This scattered the last remnants of Spanish power in Chile and cleared the way for Chilean and Peruvian independence. His life and exploits helped inspire C.S. Forester's Horatio Hornblower and Patrick O'Brian's Jack Aubrey.

THE FIRST POST

Send a postcard from the sleepy village of Sanquhar in the Nith Valley and you will have sent it from the oldest working post office on the planet. This tiny little building started out in 1712 as a stage on the 'Nithsdale Cross Post', where runners moving mail about the country on foot and horseback would stop. It is still going strong 300 years later, although the second counter position has been shut since lunchtime on 1 June 1843.

THE GREATEST GRANNY

'The most dangerous woman in Europe' is how Hitler described Queen Elizabeth the Queen Mother. Not because she was handy with a Sten gun, but because she did so much to boost British morale. Born Elizabeth Bowes-Lyon, she was the daughter of Scottish nobleman the Earl of Strathmore and spent much of her childhood in the family ancestral home of Glamis Castle in Perthshire. On the death of George VI she assumed her familiar title today in 1952 and would remain in that 'job' for another 50 years. The Queen Mum was certainly beloved by the public and was still out and about being 'dangerous' until a few months before her death at the grand old age of 101.

THE GLOVES ARE ON

As a nation we've always loved a good stooshie. Usually these are random affairs that for some reason always seem to happen about closing time. But we've produced a few champions of the official sort too. And it's thanks to us that modern boxing looks like it does: today in 1881 saw a new set of boxing rules that included the use of gloves, the ten-count and three-minute rounds. These were sponsored by Scottish nobleman John Douglas, the 9th Marquess of Queensberry.

REAL-LIFE LEGEND

With TV documentaries now exposing businesses and governments left, right and centre, the form has never been more popular, and it owes its existence to John Grierson from Doune. A tireless investigator of exploitation and cruelty, Grierson is considered the father of the documentary film. He even coined the term 'documentary' in the *New York Sun* today in 1926. His first film, *Drifters*, followed the hard lives of herring fishermen in the North Sea, 80 years before *Deadliest Catch* was doing exactly the same thing.

CANINE CRIME-FIGHTING

Revenue Officer Malcolm Gillespie was struggling to catch the gangs of whisky smugglers that roamed the braes of Aberdeenshire. So he trained a bull terrier to chase smugglers' horses, bite them on the nose and hold on until the petrified beast shook off its illicit load. Everyone thought he was barking mad, but the tactic (which he tried today in 1816) was successful and Gillespie had started a whole new branch of law enforcement – dog-handling. But the smugglers had the last laugh on Gillespie, who is said to have confiscated over 6,500 gallons of illicit whisky during his career, when he was hung for forgery in 1827.

UNIVERSITY CHALLENGED

With the founding today in 1495 of King's College in Aberdeen, Scotland had three universities (St Andrews and Glasgow being the first two). England, however, only had two (Oxford and Cambridge). Scotland then got a fourth, Edinburgh, in 1583, but it was the nineteenth century before England had a third. So for 250 years, Scotland had twice as many universities as England!

THE FREEZING FRIARS

Curling – or 'chess on ice' as it is known – was invented in wintry medieval Scotland because, frankly, there was bugger all else to do! There's a report of a match between two monks in the records of Paisley Abbey from today in 1541. And fair play to them – it must have been absolutely Baltic in those habits and sandals. We can also be proud to have the oldest curling club – Kilsyth was constituted in 1716 and its members are still sliding about rinks today. It's one of the few sports that we are genuinely world class at, with Rhona Martin skipping Team GB to Olympic gold in 2002.

HERIOT BEQUEATHS HOGWARTS

On his death today in 1624, goldsmith George Heriot left 25,000 pounds Scots (equivalent to tens of millions of pounds sterling today) to found a charitable school for 'puir, faitherless bairns'. Today George Heriot's flourishes as an independent school, but it still gives a free education to many fatherless children. Its amazing turreted castle-like architecture is rumoured to be the model for Hogwarts, Harry Potter's school of wizardry. Author J.K. Rowling wrote much of her early novels in a café overlooking the school.

FOUR-LEGGED FIRSTS

Scotland can be very proud of its record as a fertile breeding ground for dogs. At least 19 breeds originate here, including the Skye terrier, border collie, West Highland terrier, Scottish deerhound and bloodhound. The golden retriever was first bred in Glen Affric in the 1860s by Sir Dudley Marjoribanks, who wanted a hunting dog that loved swimming. Golden retrievers were first shown today at Crufts in 1908, where the judges were bowled over by their fine coats, athletic condition and all-round cuddliness.

THE MASTER PLANNER

14

Sir Patrick Geddes from Ballater was a brilliant biologist and geographer whose ideas helped him become the 'Father of British town planning'. Geddes saw the harshness of life in Edinburgh's cramped Old Town and designed towns that were more organic and green. He coined the term 'conurbation' and created the master plan for the modern city of Tel Aviv, which was approved today in 1929. And no, he wasn't responsible for Glenrothes.

OCH YOU (FORGOT ABOUT ME)

A film producer offered a barely famous Glasgow band the chance to record a song for a low-budget teen comedy film. Bryan Ferry and Billy Idol had already said no to the track, and the band only reluctantly agreed, knocking it out in three hours one afternoon. They forgot about it for six months until *The Breakfast Club* came out today in 1985 and 'Don't You (Forget About Me)' rocketed to No. 1 worldwide. Luckily Simple Minds had a few top tunes of their own up their sleeves...

WEEL DONE INDEED

Built on the Clyde, the famous tea clipper *Cutty Sark* was one of the world's fastest ships when her maiden voyage began today in 1870. In 1874 she set a record time of 73 days from London to Sydney and regularly overtook steam ships. She was named after the antics of the witch Nannie Dee in Robert Burns' 1791 poem 'Tam o' Shanter'. The saucy sight of Nannie dancing in her too-short (cutty) slip (sark) causes Tam to shout, 'Weel done, Cutty-sark!'

KELPIES WIN BY A HEAD

Created by sculptor Andy Scott, the Kelpies are one of the most exciting public artworks in the world. These gargantuan horses' heads tower a mighty 30m (half as tall again as the Angel of the North) above the Forth & Clyde canal near Falkirk, in tribute to the mighty workhorses that once powered local industry. First tossing their manes today in 2013, the Kelpies are named after the Celtic water-horse spirits that haunt Highland waters, not because they enjoy grazing on seaweed.

FLYING THE FLAG, ANY FLAG

Today in 1776 John Paul Jones (the Scottish sailor, not the bass player in Led Zeppelin) sailed on the maiden cruise of a US Navy ship, *Alfred*, and hoisted the first US ensign over a naval vessel. He later led several piratical voyages against Britain, which earned him hero status in the revolutionary United States. He advised Congress on the drawing up of navy regulations and the training of naval officers, and became known as 'Father of the US Navy'. A man of negotiable loyalty, he later became an admiral in the Russian Navy.

SMOLLETT'S SAUCY STYLE

Who is Scotland's best novelist – Scott, Stevenson, Welsh? Well, according to George Orwell it is Tobias Smollett. Born in Renton, Smollett tried his hand at being a naval surgeon before deciding on literature. He may be little read now, but his first book *Roderick Random* (published today in 1748) was a bestseller and he followed it with a string of other successes. His picaresque tales were beloved by the young Charles Dickens, perhaps because they were stuffed with adventure, violence, drinking and bed-hopping.

GREYFRIARS BOBBY PLAYS DEAD

Has there ever been a greater loyalty than that shown by Bobby the Skye terrier? The story goes that when his master passed away today in 1858, the wee doggie lay down on the grass by the grave in Greyfriars Kirkyard and could not be moved for 14 years. Of course, another tale runs that he was just a stray mutt who picked a random spot then stayed because the locals thought he was cute and brought him food. But hey, it brings the tourists flocking, so we'll stick with the first version.

A STEREOTYPICALLY INVENTIVE SCOT

In the days when every letter of every page of a book had to be put in place by hand, printing was costly and labour-intensive. Then an Edinburgh goldsmith called William Ged had the idea of taking a cast of whole pages of set type. Each page could then be reprinted, freeing up the expensive metal letters for another job. He patented this process, stereotyping, today in 1725 and it radically changed the way books were reprinted. If he'd been around today, he'd probably have invented the McKindle!

AYE SPY

Allan Pinkerton was *the* great American private eye. In 1849 he was the first detective in Chicago and in the 1850s his Pinkerton National Detective Agency caught the public eye by solving a series of train robberies. (This agency is still in existence today.) He pioneered the investigative techniques of 'shadowing' a suspect and undercover work, and became super-famous when he foiled a plot to assassinate President-elect Abraham Lincoln. Interestingly, this great law-abiding American was born in the Gorbals and only immigrated to the US aged twenty-three after marrying his fifteen-year-old bride and being wanted by the Glasgow police for his Chartist activities.

BEEF TO A T

Bovril has kept generations of football fans toastie on the terraces, but the drink actually became popular during a more deadly contest. Roslin-born John Johnston originally concocted his beefy gloop while working as a butcher in Edinburgh, concentrating discarded meat trimmings into a viscous stock. Yum. Sales really took off after Johnston secured a contract to supply the French Army in the Franco–Prussian war and he launched his company today in 1875. Bovril was then known as 'Johnston's Fluid Beef', a name that wins points for honesty if not allure.

THE MCFLYER

Today in 1923 the *Flying Scotsman* first appeared; no, not Chris Hoy – the locomotive. This beast of a train won worldwide fame for becoming the first engine to top 100mph, and being able to run between London and Edinburgh – at 392 miles then the longest express route in the world – nonstop and on time. Regrettably, history has not recorded whether its buffet car carried McEwan's Export.

THE FIRST OF MANY F-WORDS

Johnstone-born Gordon Ramsay was a talented footballer who hoped to play for Rangers until a nasty knee injury ended that dream forever. However, it turned out he had another talent – swearing at people (while doing a bit of cooking on the side). Today in 1999 he first appeared on the documentary *Boiling Point* as he prepared to open his first restaurant. Three Michelin stars later he's the Scot to turn to for a slap-up meal... and if you need someone given a bollocking on TV!

TOASTIE TOES

You probably know that Helensburgh boffin John Logie Baird created television (and if you don't, you will when you reach 2 October). But surely his most visionary achievement was his earlier invention of thermal socks, today in 1916. The 'Baird Undersock' was a cotton sock infused with borax to combat wet and cold feet, which Baird suffered from. Maybe they didn't work that well: Baird solved his own cold feet problem by sailing off to Trinidad for a while to sell some of his other innovations.

THE PUCK STOPS HERE

Modern ice hockey formally began in Montreal, with the first rules being published today in 1877. But the game itself is much older than that, and derives from Scots immigrants playing shinty on Canada's frozen lakes. Scots teams played a game in 1800 at Windsor in Nova Scotia. We also invented shinty, of course, and have played that game since before the start of recorded history.

THE COVENANTERS SIGN ON

When King Charles I introduced the Book of Common Prayer to Scotland in 1637 it unleashed fury. Scots generally didn't like the State messing with their church, and signed the National Covenant today in 1638 to state that fact. Ultimately, this led to the civil war that cost Charles his head. But over the following decades the 'Covenanters' were persecuted, with as many as 18,000 being killed from 1661 to 1680. Today they have a near-heroic status as fighters for their religious freedom. Mel Gibson will surely be making a film about them soon.

LEAP YEAR PROPOSAL

Over the centuries, the tradition of women proposing to their beloved, has been attributed to many notable historical figures. The most popular of all, perhaps, was that Queen Margaret of Scotland issued a law that fined men who turned down any marriage proposals by their partners on 29 February – date that only happens every four years. Of course, many historians have squashed this theory for two reasons. One, Queen Margaret lived quite far away in Norway at the time. And two, she would have only been five years old. This 'indecent proposal' is thought not to have become commonplace until the nineteenth century.

MARCH

OKAY DOKEY, NO HOKEY SMOKIES

Europe's culinary capitals have created some of the greatest delicacies known to man: champagne, Parma ham, Roquefort cheese – and, of course, the Arbroath smokie. Really, it's true – as of today in 2004 the humble smokie is up there with the best of them as a Protected Food Name under EU designation. A true smokie must be made within eight kilometres of the town and smoked in the traditional manner. And although the EU have for some reason failed to specify this, you should also eat it on a harbour wall with the sea wind tousling your hair and the waves crashing at your feet... mmmm, delicious!

TO THE FORE

The Scots needed a game that you could play even if the ground was hilly and one that didn't have to be cancelled if deer were wandering about the pitch. So we came up with golf. The Old Course at St Andrews may be the spiritual home of the game, but officially the oldest course is Musselburgh Links, which has a documented history dating from today in 1672. Scotland is the country with the most golf courses per capita, with 9,379 people per course. We have quite a lot of deer too, but they stay off the greens these days.

PRESLEY AT PRESTWICK

Prestwick Airport can forever glory in the fact that it's the only part of the United Kingdom Elvis Presley ever visited. Mind you, this wasn't because of any particular fondness for South Ayrshire; rather that the US Army plane carrying him home from Germany stopped to refuel there today in 1960. Elvis shook the hands of fans, signed autograph books, posed for pictures – then bewilderedly whispered to an Air Force lieutenant: 'Where am I?'

THE FORTH THAT'S A FIRST

The Forth Bridge isn't just a Scottish landmark, it's a wonder of the modern engineering world. The first major structure in Britain to be built of steel (64,800 tons of it), it's 1.6 miles long and stands 330ft tall. When opened today in 1890 it had the longest single cantilever span of any bridge in the world. It's incredibly strong and engineers predict it will still be standing 100 years from now. Which is more than can be said for the road bridge...

OUR GOAL IS TO HELP PEOPLE

Edinburgh's Mel Young, who founded the *Big Issue* magazine in Scotland, also came up with the idea for the Homeless World Cup today in 2001, while searching for an inspiring way to unite homeless people around the world. The first event kicked off two years later in Graz, Austria. Brilliantly, Scotland have achieved success in the event that our other national side can only dream of, becoming World Champions not once but twice, in 2007 and 2011.

PUTTING SCOTLAND ON THE MAP

The Bartholomew family of Edinburgh map-makers pretty much created the modern atlas. John Bartholomew Jr was the first to use layers of colours, with low ground shown in shades of green, higher ground in shades of brown, and mountains in purple and finally white. His son John George brought the name 'Antarctica' into popular use, and adopted red as the colour for the British Empire. His son (also called John) created maps for *The Times Atlas of the World*, which was first published today in 1920 and still sets the gold standard for atlases.

BELL RINGING

Alexander Graham Bell's mother and wife were both deaf-mutes, and while many men might be grateful for the peace and quiet that this brought, the Edinburgh-born inventor dedicated his life to improving communication methods for people with hearing loss. Though Bell went on to later invent the microphone, his early inventions weren't world-shattering – he managed to teach his Skye terrier to growl, 'How are you, Grandma?'. Not a great start, but today in 1876 he made up for this when he pulled an absolute corker out of the bag – he patented the telephone.

HOLE-Y WOMAN

Elaine Davidson runs an aromatherapy shop in Edinburgh, and is also the world's 'Most Pierced Woman' according to Guinness World Records. In May 2000, she had 462 piercings, 192 of them in her face. By 2005 she had slotted in a total of 3,950 body piercings, including 500 in her genitalia. By today in 2012 she had 9,000 and counting. In 2011 she married Douglas Watson, a local civil servant. He has no piercings. It probably takes her quite a while to get through airport security.

ECONOMIC WITH THE TRUTH

Adam Smith's *The Wealth of Nations* is the first modern work of economics and one of the most influential books ever published (today in 1776). The canny Kirkcaldy laddie argued that free-market economies are inherently productive and beneficial to their societies. He became a key figure in the Scottish Enlightenment and his ideas earned him the reputation of 'the father of capitalism' – whether he would be proud of his offspring after the latest banking crisis is open to debate.

MURRAY MAKES A MINT

Jane Austen, Herman Melville, Johann Goethe, Lord Byron, Sir Arthur Conan Doyle – as well as being giants of world literature, what else do they have in common? They all owe their big break to a Scottish publisher, John Murray. He also published Darwin's *Origin of the Species*, but perhaps his biggest coup came today in 1812 when he released Lord Byron's *Childe Harold's Pilgrimage*, securing the poet's fame almost overnight.

NOTABLY SHORT OF CASH

Scotland's paper money wins the prize for being the most confusing in the world. Three banks can print it, but technically, it is not 'legal tender' and can be refused in payment of a debt in Scotland as well as England. Bank of England notes under £5 are legal tender here, but since they removed English £1 notes from circulation today in 1988, there is no paper money whatsoever that is legal tender north of the border. Notes are of course accepted, but really only have the same standing as cheques.

KICKING COMIC BOOK ASS

Ka-pow! Comic books and their movies have never been more popular, and one of the biggest names in the biz hails from Scotland's very own Gotham City – well, Coatbridge. Mark Millar is loved by fans for his thrilling work on titles including *Marvel Knights Spider-Man*, *Ultimate Fantastic Four*, *Superman*, *Wolverine* and *Wanted*. He also wrote *Kick-Ass*, the film of which premiered today in 2010. Millar's lightning skills even earned him a Guinness World Record for the Fastest Production of a Comic Book! The sequel of *Kick-Ass* is out in 2013!

MILK MONITOR

Free school milk is a simple idea that helped eliminate rickets from Britain's poor children – thanks to John Boyd Orr from Kilmaurs in Ayrshire. As an undergraduate in Glasgow, Boyd Orr was appalled by poverty in the city. He became first a doctor then a nutrition pioneer and his report 'Food, Health and Income' (published today in 1936) shocked the nation. Among other statistics it showed that half of Britain's population was under-nourished, with boys at Eton on average five inches taller than at council schools. Orr dedicated his life to the fair distribution of world food, for which he won the Nobel Peace Prize in 1949.

TOO COOL FOR SCHOOL

'Colditz in kilts' is how Prince Charles described it, but Gordonstoun in Moray is generally held by neutral observers to be one of the world's best schools – if you can afford that sort of thing. It was founded today in 1934 and has produced several other notable alumni including film director Duncan Jones (son of David Bowie) and Roy Williamson of the Corries, composer of 'Flower of Scotland'. Lara Croft, of *Tomb Raider* fame, went there in her fictional childhood.

RAGGED SCHOOL-TROUSERED PHILANTHROPIST

Thomas Guthrie was a celebrated preacher and philanthropist from Brechin who in March 1847 founded a 'Ragged School' in Edinburgh's Castle Hill. This charitable institution offered free education to destitute children and the idea was taken up all over Britain. In the next eight years over 200 free schools for poor children were established and 300,000 children went through the London Ragged Schools alone between 1844 and 1881. Although I don't suppose every single one of those kids was grateful for having a school to go to...

LISTER CLEANS UP

Before Joseph Lister, surgeon's coats were stiff with dried blood; in fact, dirty coats were seen as a sign of a surgeon's knowledge. But when Lister was working at the Glasgow Royal Infirmary he realised that filthy operating conditions might be the cause of the infections that killed so many patients. After successfully treating the wounded leg of a boy with carbolic acid solution he published his findings in *The Lancet* today in 1867. Carbolic acid became the first widely used antiseptic in surgery and – though he was never paid for it – Listerine mouthwash was named in his honour.

HERE'S TO THE IRISH

This being St Patrick's Day, you should celebrate your Scottishness with a glass of Jameson's Irish whiskey. What's that you say, wrong country? Ah, but John Jameson was a Scottish lawyer from Alloa. He only settled in Dublin after marrying into the Haig whisky family, who had interests there. When Jameson bought the Bow Street Distillery in 1780, it was producing 30,000 gallons of spirit a year. A century later it was producing a million gallons a year.

PROUD TO BE PALE

When brewer Robert Disher launched his hoppy Edinburgh Pale Ale today in 1821, it was an instant hit. It turned out that the capital's hard water produced particularly delicious pale ale and by the mid nineteenth century the city had 40 breweries and was one of the foremost brewing centres in the world. Pale ale was exported in huge quantities and became known as the 'lifeblood of Empire' as it quenched the thirst of Brits in colonies worldwide.

THE TIME LORD

In the early nineteenth century local areas kept their own times according to the sun's position, which didn't matter as it took so long to get anywhere. As train journeys made long-distance travel possible, though, this discrepancy became highly inconvenient: travel any distance and you had to reset your watch. The UK solved its internal problems with the introduction of 'Railway Time' in the 1840s, but in the larger land masses problems still prevailed. Kirkcaldy-born Sandford Fleming had left Scotland for Canada and become chief engineer of the Canadian Pacific Railway. He proposed the creation of Standard Time with worldwide time zones to harmonise timetables and make travelling easier. His idea was eventually enacted today in 1918.

THE DUNCE FROM DUNS

Poor old John Duns Scotus has given his name to a word for nitwit – dunce – despite being regarded as one of the greatest of medieval thinkers. The thirteenth century Franciscan friar from Berwickshire wrote highly influential philosophy and theology. But by the sixteenth century his teachings had fallen from favour and his followers, the Dunses, were considered stupid. Still, at least Pope John Paul II thought Scotus worth being proud of when he beatified him today in 1993.

UP FOR THE CUP

When Queen's Park scrounged £56 and 13 shillings from the seven other footie clubs in existence in Scotland to pay for a cup and some medals, they didn't realise they were creating history. The inaugural Scottish Cup final took place at Hampden today in 1874, with Queen's Park beating Clydesdale 2–0. The same bit of silverware is played for today, making it the oldest trophy in Association Football and the oldest national football trophy in the world. The 1937 cup final drew 147,365 fans – also a world record.

LIVING ON A PRAYER

St Brendan was Irish but, being the patron saint of sailors, he got about a bit and founded a monastery on Eileachan Naoimh in the Garvellach Islands, Argyll. He did this around 542 AD, and parts of the chapel are still standing, making it the oldest church building of any type in the whole of Britain. His feast day was traditionally today. Not that the man himself did much feasting – his monkish diet was mostly seabird eggs and roast seaweed.

'BEND ZE KNEES, SHERLOCK'

If you've ever hit a heathery patch at Glenshee and catapulted yourself into a stupid wooden fence you'll have a hard time believing that Scotland has pioneered anything at all in the skiing world. But when Sir Arthur Conan Doyle, author of the Sherlock Holmes tales, was wintering in Switzerland for his wife's health, he had skiing boards imported from Norway. Today in 1894 the tweed-clad Scot became one of the first people ever to ski in the Alps when he crossed the 8,000ft Maienfelder Furka pass between Davos and Arosa. His run was heather-free.

VICE CITY

With supercool action set in American-style cities and Hollywood stars providing voice talent, *Grand Theft Auto* is one of the most glamorous, and successful, video game series of all time. Odd, then, that the whole thing started in Dundee. Now called Rockstar North and based in Edinburgh, the company began designing the game today in 1995. Mind you, it's a good job they did set the game overseas – it wouldn't have been quite so awesome driving round the big bad streets of Tayside.

THE BRIGHTEST SPARK

William Murdoch was a self-taught engineering genius who left Ayrshire to work mechanical wonders for James Watt's company. He perfected a method of producing gas from coal and his house was the first ever to be lit by gas. Today in 1802 he publicly demonstrated his gas lighting in London, brilliantly illuminating a factory with gas jets, to the astonishment of all present. Twenty years later most towns in Britain were lit by gas. He also developed the compressed-air message tube; Harrods used one of his systems until the 1960s.

BAD HEALTH GOES UP IN SMOKE

Scotland was the first part of the UK (and one of the first countries in the world) to adopt a ban on smoking in public places today in 2006. Since then there has been a 10 per cent drop in the country's premature birth rate, among many other health benefits. Of course, the number of grumpy-looking smokers standing outside pubs in the rain has risen exponentially, but you can't win them all.

NICE TRY, ENGLAND

The first-ever international rugby match wasn't at Twickenham or Murrayfield, but at Raeburn Place, Edinburgh Academicals' club ground, today in 1871. This 20-a-side game wasn't just the first international rugby match but the first international of any form of football. While England may have looked better, wearing white jerseys with a red rose, Scotland, for some odd reason, wore brown jerseys and white cricket flannels, it was Scotland who triumphed over the Auld Enemy, scoring a try and a goal to England's sole try.

'RIGHT, WHO FANCIES A GOOD PUNCH-UP?'

For 373 years, a Scottish infantry regiment was the most senior in the whole British Army. The Royal Scots were first formed today in 1633 when Charles I asked Sir John Hepburn for 1,200 boisterous lads to go and sort out a wee spot of bother he was having with the French. This they did, and they went on to serve with distinction in almost every army campaign in British history, including Waterloo, Sevastopol, Gallipoli and the Gulf, before merging with other regiments in 2006. Maybe we *are* always looking for trouble...

SCREW YOU, SMITH

After losing his father at sea, Robert Wilson from Dunbar maintained a strange fascination for the ocean. He became an apprentice joiner and one day, while idly watching a windmill, he had an idea. He worked on his project passionately, nearly bankrupting himself, and in 1828 his design for the first practical screw propeller was trialled on the Union Canal. Alas, short-sighted Admiralty bigwigs rejected his ideas and English inventor Francis Smith later obtained a patent. However, Wilson eventually got his due: today in 1880 the War Office granted the seventy-seven-year-old £500 in recognition of his work on the screw propeller. Better late than never, I suppose...

IT'S KENT, YE KEN

The beautiful beach at Broadstairs in Kent – runners bursting their lungs, feet pounding into the surf, Vangelis' famous music swelling ... the scene from *Chariots of Fire* (which premiered today in 1981) has to be one of the best-known in cinema. Only the famous beach isn't in Kent at all – the scene was filmed at West Sands, St Andrews. And if they had gone slightly astray and run over the Old Course like that they'd have had irate golfers flinging 3-irons at them.

SCURVY SURVEY

31

James Lind from Edinburgh was ship's surgeon on HMS *Salisbury* when he carried out one of the first clinical experiments in the history of medicine. He treated groups of sailors suffering from scurvy with different diets: some had oranges, some had cider, and one unlucky group was given a mixture of garlic, mustard and horseradish. Lind published his results today in 1753, proving that citrus fruit cured scurvy. He also established hospital ships and improved cleanliness and ventilation for sailors – essential really, considering what he was feeding them.

APRIL

LORD OF THE WEEKEND WARRIORS

As Secretary of State for War in 1908 (they were more honest about job titles in those days), Richard Haldane from Edinburgh introduced reforms to ready Britain's forces for the war that was clearly in the post. And so today Mr Haldane created the very first Territorial Army. This volunteer reserve seemed at first like a fun way to earn extra cash in peacetime, but proved a different story when you were stuck for months at a time in a rat-infested trench with Germans shooting at you.

RADAR ROB

When rumours reached the Air Ministry that Nazi Germany had a 'death ray' capable of flattening cities using radio waves, they asked Scottish scientist Robert Watson-Watt to investigate. He concluded that the 'death ray' was science fiction, but the idea of using radio waves to locate enemy aircraft could be turned into science fact. Within a few weeks he had created a working model of the world's first radar system (patented today in 1935), a device that would help the Allies win the Second World War.

THE HIGHEST OF HIGH-FLIERS

Today in 1933, Govan-born David McIntyre (the first owner of Prestwick Airport) and the then Duke of Hamilton became the first aviators to fly over Mount Everest. They piloted their Westland biplanes over the southern summit, clearing the ridge by, as the Duke said, 'a more minute margin than I cared to think about, now or ever'.

ROCK OF AGES

The world began in Edinburgh. At least, our understanding of its physical history certainly did. James Hutton was a Scottish physician and chemist who was studying some rocks on Arthur's Seat when he realised that younger volcanic rock was protruding through an older sedimentary section. This convinced him there had been a slow evolution of the earth's surface, not the 6,000-year development implied by the Bible. Today in 1785 he put his revolutionary ideas to the Royal Society and created the modern science of geology.

WHISKY GETS IN ON THE ACT

Alcohol aficionados worldwide agree there's nothing quite like a Scottish single malt. But whisky only became widely available thanks to the Excise Act passed today in 1823, which eased restrictions on licensed distilleries. Then, when the phylloxera bug destroyed France's wine and cognac production in 1880, Scotch whisky stepped into the gap. Our national spirit became internationally popular and has never looked back.

HIGHLAND FLINGERS

Scottish Highland Games are today enjoyed all over the world, and their events of shot putt and hammer throw feature in the Olympic Games. Indeed, Baron Pierre de Coubertin saw a display of Highland Games at the Paris Exhibition of 1889, which helped inspire his revival of the Olympics today in 1896. Of course, it's not just our events they need to copy – who doesn't think the Olympics would be better with bagpipes?

THE DRIVER'S DRIVER

Jim Clark was the Fife farmer's son who won two Formula 1 World Championships in 1963 and 1965. Modest, charismatic and hugely talented, he could drive pretty much anything, also winning the 1964 British Touring Car Championship and the Indy 500 in 1965. When he died in a crash at Hockenheim today in 1968 he had more Grand Prix victories (25) and more pole positions (33) than any other driver. On his gravestone, epitomising his humility, he is first marked as a farmer.

REAPING THE BENEFITS

The reaping machine invented by the Reverend Patrick Bell of Forfarshire in 1828 kick-started the mechanisation of farming. His machine had two important features still used in modern combine harvesters: rotating paddles to gather the crop and scissor-like blades to shear the stems. The devout Bell never patented his machine, believing his invention should benefit all mankind. Several American inventors were not so noble and went on to make hay with the idea. Nevertheless, Bell's brilliance was finally recognised today in 1867, two years before his death, with a £1,000 prize from the Highland and Agricultural Society of Scotland.

THE HEIGHT OF AMBITION

Dave MacLeod climbed Dumbarton Rock today in 2006. So what, you say, there's a set of steps up the back. Ah, but Dave went via a route on the rock's sheer face called 'Rhapsody'. It had taken him two solid years of attempts and several serious falls to finally master. The route was graded at E11 7a (a technical climbing measure, roughly equivalent to 'totally bloody impossible'), making it the world's hardest rock climb.

APRIL

THE SPORT OF KINGS?

10

If you thought football kicked off in nineteenth century England, think again. The game was actually popular in Scotland's medieval courts. Today in 1497 King James IV paid two shillings for a bag of 'fut ballis', and a leather-bound pig's bladder found in Stirling Castle has been dated to 1540. It is officially the world's oldest football and was discovered lodged in the rafters where presumably some overexcited marquess punted it.

DAISY DIGS UP HISTORY

11

The Lewis Chessmen are world famous for being one of the few examples of a medieval chess set. Carved from walrus ivory in the twelfth century, the 78 pieces were discovered in Uig bay on Lewis and first exhibited today in 1831. They are exquisite pieces of both art and history, showing that culture around the North Sea was flourishing at the time. Interestingly, the pieces weren't excavated by an archaeologist but by a cow rooting around in a sandbank with its horns.

HE'S GOT SOME BOTTLE

Usually it's old IRN-BRU bottles that you find floating about our waters. But today in 2012, a skipper from Shetland fished a bottle out of the North Sea that had been bobbing about for 97 years, 309 days. Released in 1914 during a marine experiment to map currents, it had drifted for a grand total of 9 nautical miles. A postcard inside promised finder Andrew Leaper a reward of sixpence for its return, and although he's still waiting for that, he does have the world record for finding the oldest message in a bottle.

GAS-TLY GHOULIES

Sunk deep under the streets of Scotland's capital is Mary King's Close, a warren of ancient streets closed off in the seventeenth century. It's one of the most haunted spots on Earth thanks to the plague victims walled up there, and it reopened today in 2003 as an attraction for spook-loving tourists. However, since this particular close was the nearest to the stagnant old Nor Loch, its famous eerie lights and hallucinogenic miasmas were more likely caused by sewage gases than ghosts.

BORDERERS ARE ON THE BALL

Everyone knows rugby kicked off in, well, Rugby, but it's a curious fact that the 'sevens' version of the game was born in Melrose. The leaner, faster form of one of the world's toughest sports was dreamed up by local butcher and ex-Melrose player Ned Haig as a way of raising funds for the cash-strapped club. The first ever sevens match was played at the Greenyards, the Melrose ground, today in 1883, with the home side beating local rivals Gala in extra time. The Melrose Sevens is still one of the sport's great events.

FOOTBALL WORLD CHAMPIONS – UNOFFICIALLY

When Scotland beat World Cup holders England today in 1967, some football fans jokingly said our national team were therefore the 'Unofficial World Champions'. In 2003 journalist Paul Brown resurrected the idea, going back to the very first international match, contested between England and Scotland in 1872, and calculating the 'world champions' on a knockout basis from then on. Astonishingly, given our lack of any normal football trophy whatsoever, Scotland are easily the most successful Unofficial World Champions, with 103 matches as champions, 13,003 days as champions and 86 title matches won, all records.

JANGLING JANSCH

One of the most influential musicians of the 1960s was a Scot who few people will have heard of – Bert Jansch. This near-genius folk guitarist has been name-checked as a major influence by Paul Simon, Donovan, Neil Young, Elton John and many folk bands. He released his self-titled album today in 1965. One of his early tunes was 'Blackwaterside', which was later 'borrowed' almost note for note by Jimmy Page and recorded by Led Zeppelin as 'Black Mountain Side'.

TREE TOPS THE LOT

If you've ever enjoyed a picnic by a fragrant pine forest, you have David Douglas from Scone to thank. This brilliant botanist arrived in America today in 1825 on one of the most successful plant-collecting trips of all time, returning with 240 new species that transformed the British landscape. These included flowers like the lupin and the penstemon and trees such as the sitka spruce, grand fir, noble fir and the mighty tree that bears his name – the Douglas fir. Britain's tallest tree is a Douglas fir in Argyll which towers 209ft, 40ft higher than Nelson's Column.

VERY FIRST AID

The St Andrew's Ambulance Association is more than just a canny way for its members to get into football matches free – it is one of the world's oldest first-aid charities. It received its Royal Charter from Queen Victoria today in 1899 and was founded in Glasgow in 1882 by a group of local doctors and businessmen who were concerned by the rapid increase in traffic accidents. What they'd make of the Clydeside Expressway is anybody's guess.

SCHOOLED IN COOL

Street trials riders make their bikes dance over the urban landscape, but today in 2009 they got a sharp lesson in how cool their sport can be. Amazingly, the hot new rider on the block wasn't from the sun-drenched California suburbs but Dunvegan in Skye. Danny Macaskill uploaded a video of bike stunts on a never-before-seen level as he jumped, flipped and flew round Edinburgh's streets. Almost overnight tens of millions had watched his gob-smacking antics and the world's most thrilling new rider had arrived.

TOM TOPS THE LOT

Forget Woods and McIlroy – golf's greatest-ever prodigy was Young Tom Morris of St Andrews (born today in 1851). He won the Open four times in a row, which no one has done since, and did so by age twenty-one. He first triumphed aged seventeen, making him still the youngest major champion in the sport. His is the first name on the famous Claret Jug. He hit the first hole-in-one in any tournament, making him also the first golfer to have to buy a round for the entire clubhouse.

A BRUSH WITH FAME

In 1992, an ex-miner from Methil called Jack Hoggan painted a scene of a couple dancing on a windy beach. He had the cheek to submit it to the Royal Academy Summer exhibition, and it was duly rejected. Twelve years later on this day the same picture, 'The Singing Butler', sold for £744,500. This piece of art now shifts more posters and postcards than any other image by any other artist in the UK and Jack Vettriano (as he is now known) no longer probably wonders what the critics think of him.

PASTEUR IN THE PUB

French megastar scientist Louis Pasteur was in Edinburgh today in 1884 for the university's tercentenary celebrations. His techniques for killing bacteria (pasteurisation) prevented the decay of beer, for which the capital's thriving brewing industry was hugely grateful. Pasteur was hosted by the Younger family (of Tartan Special fame) and toured the Holyrood Brewery to see his advances in action. The Youngers in turn were so impressed with Pasteur that they bequeathed money for a new Professorship in Public Health at the university, the first of its kind in Britain.

YEW KILLED JESUS

In the churchyard of the sleepy village of Fortingall in Perthshire is an ancient yew tree. Make that *very* ancient – the tree may be 5,000 years of age, making it the oldest tree in Europe. Local legend says that Pontius Pilate was born in its shade and played there as a child, thanks to his father's posting within the Roman Empire. Isaac Newton worked out that today in 34 AD was when Pilate ordered the crucifixion of Jesus. Not very Christian of him.

END OF THE LINE

Today in 1965 the beautiful long-distance path the Pennine Way was formally opened. But hang on – surely the Pennines are in England? Well, the trail may start at Edale in the Peak District, and run north for 267 miles through the Yorkshire Dales and the Northumberland National Park, but it actually finishes at Kirk Yetholm over the border in Scotland.

COLD BUT COOL

Babes, barrels and boards – when it comes to surfing, Thurso near John O'Groats has it all. Except bikinis, maybe. The mighty swells powering down from Arctic waters produce some of the best waves in the world. Today in 2006, Thurso successfully hosted the O'Neill Highland Open, a '5 Star' event that ensured the town ranked alongside surf meccas such as Oahu, Hawaii and Santa Cruz. Unsurprisingly, Thurso holds the world record for the coldest waters to have the competition in, being officially rated 'knacker-numbingly cold'.

WIZARD OF AUS

Lachlan Macquarie from the island of Ulva became a major-general in the British Army before being appointed Governor of New South Wales today in 1809. The colony was then just a shabby prison camp and it was largely thanks to Macquarie's reforms that the country of Australia came into being at all. He introduced the first local currency, encouraged convicts to settle as workers and established the street layouts for the modern cities of both Hobart and Sydney. Macquarie was even the first person to officially use the name 'Australia', in 1817.

THE SCOTTISH SAMURAI

Thomas Blake Glover is unknown in his homeland, but has heroic status in Japan. He helped industrialise the country, introducing the first steam train, developing the first coal mine and building the first dry dock. Glover commissioned one of the first warships in the Imperial Japanese Navy (completed today in 1869) and helped found the shipbuilding company that would later become Mitsubishi. He also helped found the Kirin Brewery. Next time you drink a Kirin, look at the mythical creature on the label; its moustache is based on Glover's.

THE ORIGINAL TEA PARTY

India's huge tea plantations only exist thanks to two Scots. Hugh Falconer from Forres was a botanist who first proposed the idea (today in 1834) that the Chinese tea plant could be successfully cultivated in India. The job itself was handled by Robert Fortune of Berwickshire, who disguised himself as a Chinese mandarin to smuggle out tea plants. Fortune's plants thrived in Indian soil, and were bred with Assam tea to make some of the finest teas the world has ever seen – and a fortune for the East India Company.

WHAT'S ANOTHER WORD FOR 'THESAURUS'?

Peter Mark Roget wasn't the happiest of children and he found that making lists of words and other things helped him feel less depressed. He took this to a new level throughout his time studying medicine at the University of Edinburgh, and his odd hobby finally came to fruition today in 1852 when he published his eponymous thesaurus. It was reprinted 28 times in his lifetime, which perhaps made him at least a little happy. Or cheerful, jovial, exultant...

ASHES TO ASHES

Thomas Carlyle was an exceptional essayist, philosopher and novelist, and possibly the world's most patient man. When he had completed his epic *History of the French Revolution*, he sent it to his mentor John Stuart Mill, whose parlour maid thought it was waste and burned it on the fire. Carlyle rewrote the whole work again. Good job, too – Charles Dickens used the book as his major source for *A Tale Of Two Cities* (published today in 1859), one of the bestselling novels of all time, with over 200 million copies sold.

BELTANE IS BELTING

1

Today will dawn as 15,000 are still enjoying a bonfire and other festivities at the Beltane Fire Festival in Edinburgh. Ostensibly a proud Celtic celebration marking the return of summer, it's also a great excuse to get wrecked, get your kit off and prance about a hilltop all night with a bunch of other happy nutters.

PINS FROM PAISLEY

It can be no coincidence that a Scotsman invented the fastest way to get your hands on money. Indeed, today in 1966, it was Paisley-born James Goodfellow who patented the Automatic Teller Machine (ATM) cash dispenser with numerical Personal Identification Number (PIN) keypad. The device was conceived at a time when trade unions were pressurising the big banks to give tellers Saturday mornings off, so they too could go shopping. Goodfellow's friends and family refer to ATMs as 'Jim's money machine'.

SWEET SUCCESS

Diabetes was a death sentence before John Macleod helped discover insulin. Macleod was born near Dunkeld, but it was in Canada that he worked with Frederick Banting and Charles Best on beating diabetes. Macleod first presented their findings today in 1922 and clinical trials soon showed insulin to be a miracle drug. It literally woke up comatose and nearly dead patients, treating their symptoms almost overnight. Macleod and Banting received the 1923 Nobel Prize.

POP GOES PAOLOZZI

Sculptor Eduardo Paolozzi was born in Leith to Italian parents. His 1947 collage, 'I Was a Rich Man's Plaything', was one of the trailblazing works in the Pop Art movement and the very first to show the word 'pop'. Paolozzi's big, bold statues grace several high-profile locations including the British Library, Euston station and Leith Walk. He created the mosaic walls of Tottenham Court Road tube station and, fittingly as a Pop Art pioneer, the cover of Paul McCartney's *Red Rose Speedway* album, released today in 1973.

HORSEY, HORSEY, DON'T YOU STOP

Here's one for you petrol heads to be proud of. The concept of 'horsepower' – the rate at which work is done – was coined by James Watt today in 1782. He wanted a marketing catchphrase to help mine owners understand how much work his new steam engine could do compared with their horses. Watt computed it to be 33,000 foot-pounds of work in one minute. This quaint-sounding measure still figures as a rating on your chainsaw, lawnmower, vacuum cleaner – and your hot-rod racing car, of course.

RECORD-BREAKING RECORDER

As every kid in the 1970s and 80s knew, Norris McWhirter was the resident brainbox on BBC TV's long-running *Record Breakers*. However, not many people know he was an all-round athlete himself who actually ran for Scotland in the 1950s. But his most notable achievement came today in 1954 when he acted as timekeeper at the Oxford race when Roger Bannister ran the first sub-four-minute mile.

BEING SCOTTISH CAN BE TOUGH

Sean Connery, Billy Connolly, Robert Burns – who do you think is the 'Most Scottish Person In The World'? Well, according to readers of the *Glasgow Herald* today in 2003, cheeky schoolboy Wee Jimmy Krankie merits that title. Wee Jimmie is really Janette Tough from Queenzieburn, of course, but she will still no doubt be proud to top the list. Mind you, given that C.U. Jimmy, Englishman Russ Abbot's caricature of a Scotsman, came third, it's not clear how much of an honour this really is.

ART OF BOYS

The 'Glasgow Boys' were a collection of artists who became world famous in the late nineteenth century. The group, which included John Lavery, James Guthrie, George Henry and E.A. Hornel, embraced the modern European style and rebelled against the art establishment of the day. They became the most significant British artists of their time and their global fame was sealed at the International Exhibition in Glasgow, which opened today in 1888.

SHORTBREAD'S BIG BREAK

Shortbread is a classic Scottish dessert that consists of three humble ingredients: flour, sugar and butter. But today in 2006 it broke into the biscuit big time when it was chosen as the United Kingdom's representative for Café Europe. This was an EU initiative that, for some reason, encouraged everyone in Europe to sit in cafés all day. However, despite this exposure, 95 per cent of shortbread sales are still made to grannies in Kelvinside.

SAVING SOULS

The Kirkcudbrightshire minister Dr Henry Duncan believed in helping your fellow man – and he practised what he preached. At a time of scarcity in his village he personally funded the import of corn. Duncan opened gardens for the enjoyment of all and, today in 1810, he opened the world's first commercial savings bank in Ruthwell. Its aim was to help savers get through the bad times by bringing their money together and, unusually, it paid interest to ordinary people. Within five years, savings banks based on his model were operating throughout the United Kingdom. If only bankers were so noble today...

THE BATTLING CHAPLAIN

Perthshire-born Adam Ferguson was a chaplain in the Black Watch who became a philosopher and the 'father of sociology' with his Essay on the History of Civil Society (1767). In it he attacked modern commercial society for making men weak and selfish and abandoning communal virtues. Ahead of his times, then. Thoughtful philosopher and clergyman though he was, Ferguson also found time to get stuck in at the Battle of Fontenoy against France today in 1745, drawing his sword and leading a charge on the enemy.

LIPTON LUCKS OUT

12

Thomas Lipton opened his first grocery store today in 1871 in the Gorbals, aged just twenty-one. He had a knack for publicity and kept prices keen by buying direct from producers. He built a chain of shops and founded the tea brand that still bears his name. Lipton was also yachting daft, and he tried and failed to win the America's Cup on five occasions. Still, his efforts made his brand famous in the States. Ever-cheerful in defeat, he was awarded a special cup for being 'the best of all losers'.

HIGH-FLYING HENDERSON

Lieutenant General Sir David Henderson from Glasgow was a brilliant soldier and the Army's leading authority on tactical intelligence in the early twentieth century. He fell for the new-fangled invention of aviation and in 1911, at the age of forty-nine, Henderson became the world's oldest pilot. The next year he helped set up the Royal Flying Corps, founded today. This became the Royal Air Force and Henderson was its first commander. He even had a lovely bushy moustache.

BIG IN JAPAN

Little known here, William Kinnimond Burton was an Edinburgh-born engineer who is a virtual hero in Japan. Today in 1887, Burton took up what he thought would be a temporary post on the engineering staff at Tokyo Imperial University. But Japan was then suffering several serious epidemics, particularly cholera, and Burton soon swapped academia for action. Nine years later, he had planned the modern water and drainage systems of several Japanese cities, including Tokyo. The sand filtration system he built in Shimonoseki still produces water pure enough to bottle. His picture adorns the label. He also found time to design Japan's first skyscraper and take a Japanese wife.

HOME FROM HOME

There's a corner of a foreign field that will be forever Scotland. Corby in Northamptonshire is known as 'Little Scotland' – 12,000 local residents (one in five) were born north of the border, Glasgow patter is heard everywhere and there's an annual Highland Gathering. This is thanks to the opening of a massive steelworks in the town today in 1934, which attracted a huge number of Scottish migrant workers. Now the local Asda sells 17 times more IRN-BRU than anywhere else in England.

BOSWELL'S BEST BIOGRAPHY

Samuel Johnson was England's foremost man of letters, a brilliant poet, critic and lexicographer; James Boswell was a second-rate Scottish advocate and heavy drinker. But this original 'odd couple' enjoyed a remarkable and historic friendship. And Boswell surpassed himself by writing the down-to-earth and entertaining *Life of Johnson* (published today in 1791), which is often regarded as the finest biography ever written.

THE GOOD GIRAFFE

A snapping spring morning with a brisk east wind – what you need right now is a piping hot mocha given to you, free, by a giraffe. Well, that's what Dundee-born Armstrong Baillie thought when he began his random acts of kindness today in 2012. He dressed up in a furry giraffe suit his mother made him, before doing good deeds simply because it makes him feel nice. Armstrong has cleaned up litter, handed out free bananas to marathon runners and given £10 vouchers to mums in hospitals.

THERE'S A NIP IN THE AIR TODAY

It's World Whisky Day (today in 2013), so let's celebrate what the world loves most about our country. We've been officially making the stuff since 1495 when King James IV granted Friar John Cor of Lindores Abbey in Fife 'eight bolls of malt' to make whisky – equivalent to a couple of hundred bottles. God bless those medieval monks. Today, with 108 distilleries in Scotland, you don't need royal permission to have a dram. Just go easy, or tomorrow will be World Bangin' Heid Day.

HAMISH TO THE RESCUE

Next time the news announces a successful mountain rescue, be proud it's probably thanks to Hamish MacInnes. The legendary climber was pivotal in creating the modern mountain rescue service in Scotland – he also designed the first all-metal ice axe and the 'MacInnes Stretcher', which is used for rescues worldwide. His skills as a safety adviser and stunt double have featured in films including *The Eiger Sanction*, *The Mission*, *Rob Roy* (released today in 1995) and *Highlander.*

LAUGHING ALL THE WAY TO LE BANQUE

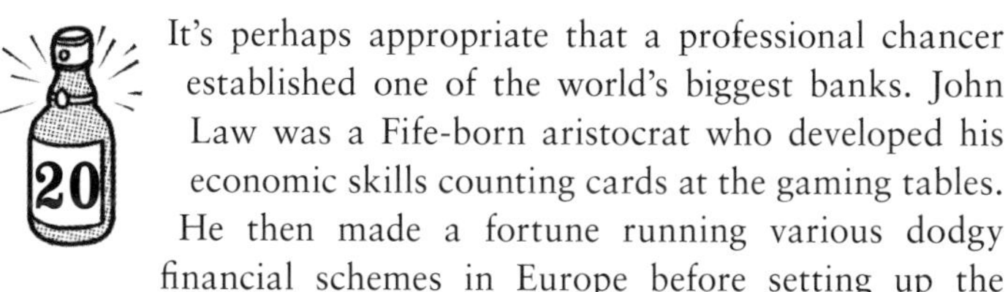

It's perhaps appropriate that a professional chancer established one of the world's biggest banks. John Law was a Fife-born aristocrat who developed his economic skills counting cards at the gaming tables. He then made a fortune running various dodgy financial schemes in Europe before setting up the Banque Générale as a de facto national bank of France today in 1716, claiming he could help the country's economy recover from years of war. This venture failed catastrophically, but Law was okay: he fled France dressed as a woman. An ancestor of a certain Mr Goodwin, maybe?

MAD, BAD AND ... SCOTTISH?

Poor old George Gordon didn't have the best start in life. Born with a club foot, he was raised alone by his alcoholic mother in Aberdeenshire (his mad, brutal, womanising father having died when he was three). Then, today in 1798, the lad's luck changed. His uncle died and the ten-year-old George inherited his title of Lord Byron. He also inherited the ancestral Byron home of Newstead Abbey and went on to become one of the English literature's most famous poets.

PORRIDGE POWERS PLASTER PROGRESS

Porridge might seem an unlikely instigator of medical progress, but it helped Dr Alexander Anderson of Glasgow become the first physician to use cotton wool. A textile worker whose child had fallen into hot porridge came to him with the child wrapped in processed cotton ready for spinning, which had been the only material to hand. Anderson saw the scalds had already begun to heal. He conducted trials with this 'cotton wool' and today in 1828 published his recommendation of its use in the treatment of burns.

FREE TO TAKE A PHOTO

Today in 1843, 121 ministers and 73 elders left the Church of Scotland to form the Free Church of Scotland. 'Just another religious spat,' you might think. But the painter David Octavius Hill was there and decided to record the scene using the new invention of photography, helped by photographer Robert Adamson. Hill and Adamson went on to pioneer the art of photography in Scotland, taking the first 'action' shots of soldiers and photos of ordinary working people. But their biggest triumph was taking the world's first-ever photo of men drinking beer.

A WHEELY GOOD IDEA

The Falkirk Wheel (opened by HM the Queen today in 2002) is the world's first and only rotating boat lift. It re-linked the Forth and Clyde Canal with the Union Canal, which had been 115ft apart vertically since 1933 when a flight of 11 locks was dismantled. This beautiful structure is so perfectly balanced that it can raise 330 tons of water – and a boat – in under five minutes using only enough electricity to power two kettles.

YOUR MOTHER WAS A HAMSTER AND YOUR FATHER SMELLED OF ELDERBERRIES

Doune Castle is a medieval stronghold and place of pilgrimage for fans of silliness. The castle minded its own business for about 500 years before becoming seriously famous when scenes for the film *Monty Python and the Holy Grail* were shot there (released today in 1975). Thirty years later, organisers of the first 'Monty Python Day' were blown away when thousands of coconut-clutching fans turned up at the castle gates demanding to see the Holy Grail. Historic Scotland now issues tickets for the event, rather than forcing visitors to enter the castle in a giant Trojan rabbit.

BLACK'S BRILLIANCE

James Black from Uddingston did well at school but his family was far too poor to send him to university. His maths teacher persuaded him to sit the St Andrews entrance exam anyway and Black did so well he won a scholarship to study medicine. During a brilliant career he developed the beta-blocker propranolol, one of the biggest breakthroughs in twentieth century pharmacology. He was knighted in 1981, won the Nobel Prize for Medicine in 1988 and today in 2000 was appointed to the Order of Merit, Britain's highest honour.

SOME IMPRESSIVE FAX

When your alarm goes off tomorrow at daft o'clock, remember to say a word of thanks to Alexander Bain from Caithness. Bain patented the first electric clock today in 1841 and was certainly a man far ahead of his time. He proposed an 'earth battery', built from zinc and copper plates buried in the ground, and, incredibly, invented an experimental fax machine way back in 1843. Rumours that the first image he faxed was a picture of his girlfriend's ankles are untrue.

YOU'RE TAKING THE PEACE

28

Wedding preparations could begin today in 1503 after the Pope signed a Papal Bull approving the marriage of James IV of Scotland to Margaret Tudor, daughter of Henry VII of England. Also ratified that day was 'A Treaty of Perpetual Peace' between Scotland and England. It lasted 10 years, which in fairness was a lot longer than most folk would have given it.

A PHOTOGRAPHIC MEMORY

Mungo Ponton was a Scottish inventor who in 1839 was experimenting with the early photographic processes developed by William Fox Talbot. Ponton made the key discovery that sunlight makes potassium dichromate insoluble, allowing permanent prints to be produced. He presented his findings today but didn't patent his process; his ideas were taken up by others, making him one of the unsung fathers of photography – but then who'd want a father called Mungo?

MODERNIST MAESTRO

Sir Basil Spence was a Scottish modernist architect who was so talented that he was made a lecturer while still a student. He designed Glasgow Airport, the Home Office building near St James's Park in London, and the 'Beehive' – New Zealand's parliament building. The consecration of his masterpiece, the rebuilt Coventry Cathedral, was celebrated today in 1962. Unpopular at first, this is now generally held in affection. The same, alas, cannot be said of his 'Hutchie C' tower block in the Gorbals, which was blown up in 1993 to general rejoicing.

CASH IN HAND

We all have cash-flow problems from time to time. But until today in 1728, you had to solve this by begging, borrowing or stealing; no bank would have helped you out. Then the Royal Bank of Scotland allowed William Hog, an Edinburgh merchant, to take £1,000 (worth £63,664 today) more out of his account than he had in it – the world's first overdraft. Ah, but how times change! The same bank is now £45 billion overdrawn at the Bank of Joe Public.

JUNE

TOP OF THE CROPS

Several modern sports owe their success to Alexander Shanks, an engineer from Arbroath. He invented the first modern lawnmower that could do a really decent job, being able to both cut the grass closely and roll it. Shanks died young, but his son showed off the company's mowers at the Great Exhibition (today in 1851) and business flourished, particularly among sporting groundsmen. By the twentieth century Shanks's mowers were cutting the courts of Wimbledon, the cricket ground at Lord's and the Old Course at St Andrews. You might say Shanks was outstanding in his field!

TEMPLETON WAS NO WALKOVER

Snooty local residents didn't want James Templeton to build his new carpet factory on Glasgow Green, which is why Glasgow Corporation rejected design after design. So Templeton hired the architect William Leiper to produce a design so grand it couldn't possibly be binned. Leiper modelled the building on the Doge's Palace in Venice and it still looks amazing today. Templeton's was once Glasgow's biggest single employer, with 7,000 workers. Its carpets graced parliaments, concert halls, the *Titanic* and were trod by HM the Queen at her Coronation today in 1953.

THE EXCITEMENT IS IN TENTS

It's the start of National Camping Week and many kids will be enjoying the thrill of their first night under canvas. Over the years the classic 'Vango Force Ten' has probably had more midnight feasts in it than any other tent and is still seen on mountain summits the world over. Not many people know that this famous outdoor brand is Scottish: the name Vango is an anagram of Govan, where the company started (making tents that is, not using them – Clydeside isn't renowned for its scenic splendours).

RENNIE RULES THE RIVER

It was a Scotsman who helped keep Victorian London on the move. John Rennie from East Linton was one of those genius civil engineers who we seemed able to produce at the drop of a tartan tammy. After knocking out the Lancaster, Crinan and Rochdale canals, he designed East India and West India Docks in London as well as quays in Hull, Liverpool, Greenock and Leith. Then he tried bridges. For 67 years, three Thames spans were his: Southwark, Waterloo and London bridges, and he created the first designs for old Vauxhall Bridge, which opened today in 1816.

ONE COOL DUDE

William Thomson, Lord Kelvin, was Professor of Natural Philosophy at Glasgow University for 53 years, which is good enough to make this son of Belfast an honorary Scot. Thompson helped formulate the laws of thermodynamics and made pioneering electric telegraph inventions. He was the first UK scientist to be elevated to the House of Lords and his house in Professors' Square was the first in Britain to be lit by electricity. The Kelvin temperature scale, which he proposed today in 1848 and which identifies –273.15°C as absolute zero, is named after him. Thomson took his Lordship title from the River Kelvin.

RYDER'S REAL HISTORY

6

2012 saw the greatest European Ryder Cup victory ever, with our golfers staging a heroic comeback from 10–6 down on the final day at Medinah. The first-ever Ryder Cup-style matches were played on this day in 1921 at Gleneagles golf course, Perthshire, when Great Britain beat the American golf team 9–3. The second such international contest in 1926 was won 13½–1½ by Britain, and it was after this event that seed merchant Samuel Ryder made it official by donating the trophy that now bears his name.

ULTRASOUND IS ULTRA SOUND

When war-hero Ian Donald became Professor of Midwifery at Glasgow University in 1955, he realised that the Royal Navy's sonar technology could work wonders for gynaecologists. Teaming up with a Clyde shipbuilder, Donald built a prototype scanner that he tested on lumps of steak. After successfully identifying an easily removable ovarian cyst in a woman who had been diagnosed as having inoperable cancer, he published a paper in *The Lancet* today in 1958 outlining his breakthrough. Ultrasound has since become a major aid in diagnosing foetal health, although on the down side it has led to those grainy black-and-white baby pictures that expectant fathers bore all their friends with.

BIRTH OF BIG BROTHER

1984 by George Orwell (published today in 1949) is a stone-cold classic of modern English literature. Oddly, it owes its existence to a humble farmhouse on the island of Jura. In London, Orwell was suffering from the tuberculosis that would eventually kill him. So he took himself off to a 'completely ungettable-at' place – Barnhill in the wild north of the island. Here he found the freedom and fresh air he needed to create his masterpiece of state power and mind control.

DRIVING AMBITION

When Isambard Brunel designed his SS *Great Britain* as the largest-ever vessel he discovered an equally mammoth problem: there wasn't a foundry in the country big enough to forge its immense drive shaft. So Scottish engineer James Nasmyth invented the steam hammer (patented today in 1842). Powerful enough to forge the largest pieces of metal, Naysmyth could also set it to crack an egg placed in a wine glass without breaking the glass. Ultimately the steam hammer became the driving force behind the development of heavy engineering (rather than cooking) in Britain.

QUARTER PAST PANSY

Science, engineering, the arts – Scotland has led the way in them all. Oh, and floral clocks, too, of course. The world's first petalled timepiece was invented by John McHattie and ticked into life in West Princes Street Gardens, Edinburgh, today in 1903. At first it only had an hour hand, but a minute hand was added the following year and the concept was soon underwhelming tourists all over the world.

FASTEST BAGPIPE PLAYING

Sergeant Mick Maitland of No. 111 RAF Fighter Squadron made history today in 1986 when he became the fastest bagpiper in the world. Not because his fingers were super-agile, but because he was flying at Mach 2.0 in a Phantom XV574 piloted by his squadron commander 40,000ft over Cyprus. Mick belted out 'Scotland the Brave' at full volume and his commander somehow resisted the urge to push the button on Mick's ejector seat.

HIS NAME IS UP IN LIGHTS

The world is brighter thanks to Glasgow-born chemist William Ramsay. Today in 1898 he discovered the gas neon (his son suggested the name, from the Greek for 'new'). Ramsay was on an element-discovering roll, having already identified argon and krypton. He would go on to complete his set of the 'noble' or inert gases by discovering xenon. The potential of neon's red glow when electrified was quickly discovered, and neon tubes for advertising were being sold as early as 1912.

EGGSTRAORDINARY THINKING

Kidney machines are a modern medical wonder that save thousands of lives a year. But the idea behind them first seeped into the head of Glasgow chemist Thomas Graham. He noticed that some crystalloids diffused through a semi-permeable membrane he had made from vegetable parchment coated with egg white. Graham called this process 'dialysis' and his discovery (announced today in 1861) is still the basic principle behind today's hi-tech dialysis machines. They no longer use egg whites, which given the price of eggs these days is probably a good job.

SLIPPING ON THE DOCK OF THE BAY

Thomas Morton was a Leith shipbuilder who realised that placing a ship in a dry dock for a simple repair was an unnecessary expense. So he designed a cradle on rails that allowed ships to be hauled clear of the water on a ramp for repair at a tenth of the cost of a dry dock. He completed the first 'patent slip' at Bo'ness today in 1821, and within 10 years a further 44 had been constructed around the country, revolutionising the repair of vessels and cleaning more dirty bottoms than a new mother.

THEY STUCK THE LANDING

Born in Glasgow, Arthur Brown was the navigator of the first successful nonstop transatlantic flight, completed today in 1919. Brown and his pilot John Alcock had left Newfoundland 16 hours earlier and flown 1,980 miles in their modified Vickers Vimy bomber. They were presented with a £10,000 prize by the Secretary of State for Air, Winston Churchill, and were also knighted. Alas, their plane was damaged on landing – what appeared to be a nice green field from the air turned out to be a Galway bog!

HIS PEN WAS MIGHTIER THAN HIS SAW

Robert Thomson from Stonehaven was Scotland's Edison. Brilliant but batty, he invented the fountain pen (first exhibited today in 1851), the ribbon saw, the pneumatic tyre (43 years before Dunlop), the road steamer and the portable steam crane (which he forgot to patent). Aged seventeen he got in trouble with his mum for deconstructing her mangle; she was, however, delighted when he rebuilt it to an improved design that could work twice as fast.

THE ORIGINAL WHIZ KID

Sir Keith Elphinstone from Musselburgh was an ingenious electrical engineer who invented several types of car speedometer. He also installed the original electric speed recording equipment at the world's first purpose-built motorsport venue, Brooklands (opened today in 1907). The world land speed record set there in 1909 was the very first to utilise electronic timing. In the First World War Elphinstone used his skills to develop super-efficient sighting equipment for naval guns, making the job of blowing up the enemy that much easier.

EWART MAKES AN EAGLE ON THE 18TH

Charles Ewart from Kilmarnock was an ensign in the Scots Greys when he single-handedly captured a French regimental eagle at the Battle of Waterloo, today in 1815. Ewart killed several enemies to get the emblem, and its capture demoralised the French. Only two French Eagles were captured in the whole 100-day Waterloo campaign. Ewart was hailed a hero but was rather modest – invited to speak at a celebratory dinner by Sir Walter Scott, he begged to be excused, saying that he 'would rather fight the Battle of Waterloo over again, than face so large an assemblage'.

MAP MAKER EXTRAORDINAIRE

Next time you're up a hill swearing at your map because a bridge it says is there most definitely isn't, take a deep breath and be proud that the map in your hands (and virtually every other map in this country) owes its existence to Scottish military engineer William Roy. After the Jacobite Rebellion of 1745, George II demanded an accurate survey of the Highlands. Roy's success with this led to a new job: the first triangulation of the whole of Britain, and today in 1784 he measured the baseline between Hampton and Heathrow. His work eventually led to the founding of the Ordnance Survey in 1791.

FOUNTAIN MAKES A SPLASH

It's big, orange, wet and a famous symbol of Glasgow – no, not a 3-litre bottle of IRN-BRU, but the Doulton Fountain. Designed to mark Queen Victoria's Golden Jubilee (today in 1887) it is 46ft high and 70ft wide, making it the largest terracotta fountain in the world. If only it flowed with ginger...

ORKNEY'S A DIVE

Scapa Flow in Orkney has always been one of the world's great natural harbours, with room for several navies. The defeated German fleet was gathered there at the end of the First World War, until today in 1919 when its commander scuttled every ship, sending 52 vessels to rest on the shallow sandy seabed. This colossal act of littering was then considered dishonourable and a waste of good ships. But now the wrecks give Orkney some of the best scuba diving on the planet.

PUT A MAC ON YOUR BACK

Considering the state of our weather, it really is no surprise that a Scot invented the waterproof coat. Charles Macintosh was a successful chemist who dissolved rubber using naphtha and used it to create a waterproof, flexible fabric (patented today in 1823). Early macs tended to smell and melt a bit in hot weather, but were still popular. He fitted out an 1824 Arctic expedition and also made the first inflatable lifejacket and first rubber airbed.

IF IT WASNAE FOR YOUR WELLIES...

It all kicked off for the Hunter Boot Company today in 1856, when its founders established a rubber goods factory in Edinburgh. The company later hit the big time by designing a wellington boot that could stand up to the mud of First World War trenches, eventually making more than a million pairs for Britain's soldiers. Today, it lives on as maker of the ubiquitous green wellies, which are essential wear for farmers, outdoor types and festival-goers, plus fashionistas who for some reason want sweaty feet in the city.

BATTERING AT BANNOCKBURN

You don't have to be a fervent nationalist to be impressed by the Scottish performance at Bannockburn. It started with Robert the Bruce cleaving Henry de Bohun's head in two with his battleaxe and ended the next day with a Scottish force of around 7,000 men routing an English army of 22,000 on this day in 1314. A defining moment in Scottish history, it was a vital step towards retaining independence and inspired the song 'Flower of Scotland', which is something to be proud of or not, depending on your musical taste.

I WANT TO RIDE MY BICYCLE

The dandy horse was a fun two-wheeled vehicle that the rider pushed along with his feet. Then Dumfries blacksmith Kirkpatrick Macmillan realised how much better it would be if you could power it without touching the ground. So he fitted cranks and pedals and created one of the world's great inventions – the bicycle. One of his first test runs was to Glasgow, 68 miles away, today in 1842. It was a success, although it did take two days and cost him a five-shilling fine when he hit an astonished pedestrian in the Gorbals ... which sounds very painful.

LIFE'S A GAS

Joseph Black was a brilliant chemist who today in 1755 delivered a paper outlining his discovery of carbon dioxide. He also discovered latent heat and specific heat, so becoming the father of thermodynamics. Black was pals with David Hume, Adam Smith, and other stars of the Scottish Enlightenment, and was also friends with James Watt. His discovery of latent heat was a major boost to Watt's design of the steam engine, and his cash pretty much paid for Watt's research.

BIG-FOOTED BEASTIE

Clydesdale draught horses are famous for their terrific strength and used to be exported from Scotland in huge numbers. Bred in Lanarkshire to be tough as old boots, the breed was officially registered today in 1877. In the 1930s, the world's largest horse was a Clydesdale called Carnera, who stood 19 hands 1½ in high (6ft 6in at the shoulder). He hauled delivery wagons around Falkirk for the Barr's soft drinks company. It took 24in of iron bar to make one of his shoes; the average for other horses was 17.

DIAMOND GEEZER

Next time your kids are mucking about with your valuables, don't despair – be proud of their efforts. The young mineralogist George Mackenzie was a renowned home experimenter who successfully converted iron into steel by adding powdered diamonds. Published today in 1800, his findings were the first scientific proof that diamond and carbon were one and the same substance. In these experiments the resourceful baronet is said to have made liberal use of his mother's jewels.

RIVER DEEP

In 1770 the lower Clyde was known for shipbuilding but the industry had a problem: the river was still very shallow in the city – just two feet deep in parts. Then today brilliant engineer John Golborne started building the first of more than 100 jetties that helped the river scour out new deeper channels. Within a few years shipping of any size could sail right into the centre of the city. Glasgow now enjoyed all the advantages of a deep-sea harbour beside an industrial heartland. Trade boomed and shipbuilding followed: soon Clydebank became the world's pre-eminent shipbuilding centre.

ELEMENTARY, MY DEAR DAVY

Strontian in Lochaber is the only place in Britain which has an element named after it. Lead was mined here in the eighteenth century and the ore *strontianite* was discovered in the mines. The new element itself was eventually isolated by Sir Humphry Davy and announced by him in a lecture to the Royal Society today in 1808. To fit in with similar elements, he changed the name to strontium. Those unfamiliar with Scottish pronunciation can be thankful it wasn't discovered at Acharachle.

JULY

A LEVEL-HEADED LAD

James Jardine was a Scottish civil engineer who built the UK's first-ever railway tunnel, on the Innocent Railway in Edinburgh (opened today in 1831). He was also the first person to determine mean sea level, but his proudest achievement was guaranteeing that Edinburgh's booming breweries (and the general public, of course) had a plentiful supply of pure water by building Glencorse, Threipmuir and Harlaw reservoirs. Cheers, Jimmy!

HIGH-CALIBRE THINKING

Today in 1881, an assassin shot US President James Garfield, and a bullet remained lodged in Garfield's body. This was terrible news for America and Garfield himself, obviously, being flunked out in his bed gravely ill. But it did give Scotsman Alexander Graham Bell (inventor of the telephone) another chance to show his genius. In an effort to find the rogue lump of lead, Bell invented the world's first metal detector. The bullet remained unfound (the metal springs in the patient's bed didn't help) and Garfield died 19 September 1881.

IT COULD ONLY HAPPEN TO A WELDER

James Herriot, the quintessential chronicler of Yorkshire rural life, was actually called Alf Wight and brought up in Glasgow, where his father worked in the shipyards. He studied at Glasgow Veterinary College and got a job as a vet in Yorkshire today in 1940, aged twenty-four. This county then became the setting for his famous *All Creatures Great and Small* series of books. Which is fair enough, as there aren't that many cows in Govan.

'YOU COULD BE RIGHT - COME BACK IN 50 YEARS'

The world watched in wonder today in 2012 as scientists announced they had found the most sought-after thing in the world – no, not a taxi at Queen Street station – the Higgs boson. This miraculous morsel of matter creates an invisible energy field that gives everything, from planets to portions of chips, their mass. Its existence was first proposed by Peter Higgs, a physicist at Edinburgh University, in 1964. He was in the room 48 years later when experiments caught up with his thinking and proved him right.

BAA BAA CLONED SHEEP

5

Most of us can't tell two sheep apart at the best of times, but this reached a whole new level today in 1997: the world's first cloned mammal, Dolly the sheep, was born at the Roslin Institute in Midlothian. She was named after Dolly Parton because the donor cell for the cloning procedure was taken from a mammary gland.

A MOUNTAINOUS ACHIEVEMENT

The splendid Perthshire peak of Schiehallion went down (or should that be up?) in scientific history today in 1774. Solitary and symmetrical, the hill was just what the Astronomer Royal, Nevil Maskelyne, was looking for when he was trying to calculate the weight of the earth. By measuring how much the massive mountain deflected a pendulum, Maskelyne came up with a pretty accurate figure. Plus, when his assistant on the trip, Charles Hutton, needed a way to work out the hill's volume accurately, he promptly invented contour lines. Quite a productive summer holiday...

THE NOVEL NOW DEPARTING FROM PLATFORM 4...

The world doesn't have many train stations named after novels – in fact, only one. *Waverley* by Sir Walter Scott was first published today in 1814 and was phenomenally popular with critics and the public, selling out its first print run of 1,000 copies within two days. It practically created the still-popular genre of historical fiction and gave its name to Edinburgh's main terminal. The novel was named after one of its characters, but rumours that the new tram stop in Leith will be called 'Sickboy' are unfounded.

FIRST KNIGHT OF AUCHTERMUCHTY

Jimmy Shand probably got more people whirling and jigging than any other musician in history. The legendary accordionist's career spanned eight decades and he recorded more tracks than the Beatles and Elvis Presley combined. He played in some of the world's most prestigious venues, including the Carnegie Hall in New York, and today in 1999 he became the first accordionist to be knighted.

STROKE OF GENIUS

Put-put-put-put ... no, it's not a bad golfer, it's the unmistakable sound of the two-stroke engine. Glaswegian engineer Dugald Clerk exhibited the world's first successful two-stroke engine today in 1879 and patented it two years later. Its neat, powerful design made it perfect for motorboats, chainsaws and motorbikes, even if it did make them sound a bit farty.

PRETTY PATTERNS

David Brewster was a child prodigy who built a telescope aged ten and went to Edinburgh University at twelve. His primary field of study was the physics of light and he worked on the dioptic lens, hugely benefiting lighthouses. But his most famous invention was the kaleidoscope (patented today in 1817). This became the Rubik's Cube of its day, with millions being sold.

ART FOR ALL, INCLUDING RODENTS

Kelvingrove Museum was magnificent enough to start with, housing one of Europe's greatest art collections. But since it reopened today in 2006 after a major restoration, it has become not only the most popular free-to-enter visitor attraction in Scotland, but also the most visited museum in the United Kingdom outside London. Oh, and the story that the building was accidentally constructed back-to-front is a myth. The grand entrance was always intended to face the park, presumably for the benefit of the squirrels.

HE IS THE GREATEST

The greatest Canadian of all time was born in Falkirk. Tommy Douglas was a popular politician who became the Premier of Saskatchewan. After nearly having his leg amputated as a boy because his parents couldn't afford a doctor, he determined that health care should be free for all. Today in 1966 his vision was realised when Canada's version of the NHS, Medicare, came into being. In 2004 a poll named him the 'Greatest Canadian'. Douglas also found time to be a Baptist minister, a champion lightweight boxer and Kiefer Sutherland's grandfather.

OUT FOR THE COUNT

The Glasgow Coma Scale is a globally used neurological scale that gives medical staff an objective measure of impaired consciousness. A patient is assessed and given a score between 3 (deep unconsciousness or death) and 15 (fully awake). The scale was first published today in 1974. Contrary to popular belief, it was not developed by policemen studying the states of various people found on Sauchiehall Street on a Saturday morning, but by Graham Teasdale and Bryan J. Jennett, neurosurgery professors at Glasgow University.

PLAYFAIR PLAYS ABOUT

William Playfair, brother of architect James, led what could charitably be described as a colourful life. He was James Watt's assistant, but got bored so tried being a millwright, accountant, inventor, silversmith, investment broker, economist, statistician, pamphleteer, translator, publicist, land speculator and journalist. Unfortunately, he was also a convict, blackmailer and, most heinously, a banker. Playfair somehow found time to invent the line graph, the bar chart and the pie chart. He also took part in the storming of the Bastille, today in 1789.

SKIN AND BONE

Muirhead Bone isn't a painful joint condition, but a Glaswegian printer's son who trained as an architect and then became known for his etchings. He went on to achieve even more renown today in 1916 when he became Britain's first official war artist. Dispatched to the Western Front, his poignant images of the Battle of the Somme brought the realities of the war home to people. He also drew the only slightly less dangerous world of the Clyde shipyards.

CREATING THE McCURRY

Chicken tikka masala is the most popular dish in Britain, but it's about as Indian as a deep-fried Mars Bar. Apparently Ali Ahmed Aslam, a chef cooking chicken tikka in Glasgow's Shish Mahal restaurant, was infuriated when a customer complained, 'Where's my gravy?' So he knocked up a sauce with a can of tomato soup, some cream and a few spices, and slammed it down – and the customer loved it. It got official recognition of sorts today in 2009, when MP Mohammad Sarwar tabled a motion in Parliament calling for Glasgow to be given European Union Protected Designation of Origin status for the dish ... so far the EU have not been hot on the idea.

TB OR NOT TB

When John Crofton became professor of respiratory diseases at Edinburgh University in 1952, tuberculosis was running rampant. Crofton then pioneered one of the great medical breakthroughs of the twentieth century, developing a cure for TB by combining three antibiotics. This 'Edinburgh Method' (announced at the annual meeting of the BMA today in 1958) saved millions of lives and formed a model for similar combination therapies treating cancer and HIV.

THE BRU IS BORN

Today we toast our other national drink, hangover cure, modern cocktail mixer and rumoured reason for Scotland boasting the world's highest percentage of redheads – IRN-BRU. It first fizzed in Falkirk in 1901, under the name Strachan's Brew, and thirsty local foundry workers lapped it up. When legislation required the removal of the word 'brew' from the name, as the drink is not brewed, IRN-BRU was born, today in 1946. IRN-BRU has long outsold both Coca-Cola and Pepsi in its homeland, a feat that is only matched by Peru's Inca Kola.

BODY OF EVIDENCE

In the 1820s, Edinburgh's medical school was flourishing, but had one major problem: not enough cadavers for dissection. So William Burke and William Hare came up with an innovative solution – killing people. Anatomist Dr Robert Knox turned a blind eye and the 'body snatchers' came to haunt the public imagination. It took 17 murders before they were caught and Burke was hanged. But this unsavoury chapter in Scottish history did lead to the passing of the Anatomy Act today in 1832, which gave medics legal access to corpses and helped medical science leap forward.

OUR EXPLORER

When his mother died in 1774, ten-year-old Alexander Mackenzie left Stornoway for North America. He became a fur trader and today in 1793 he became the first European to cross North America from the Atlantic to the Pacific, outpacing the famous Lewis and Clark expedition by 10 years. The Mackenzie River is named after him. He certainly was a no-nonsense sort of fellow; he named his party's dog 'Our Dog'.

KING OF THE RIVER

Mungo Park might sound like a nice green spot beside Glasgow Cathedral, but he was actually a Scottish explorer who famously became the first Westerner to find the Niger River, today in 1795. Presumed dead, he finally made it home two years later and his expedition journal turned him into a superstar. Alas, he was attacked by natives and drowned on a second expedition in 1806. But you can see why he went – life in hometown Peebles must have paled after that excitement. And besides, the Tweed had already been discovered.

BULLY FOR YOU

John Bull, the plain-talking, stubborn, hard-drinking farmer in a Union Jack waistcoat with a bulldog by his side, is the archetypal image of Englishness. Ironically, he was created by a Scottish satirist called John Arbuthnot. The character first appeared today in 1712 and was Arbuthnot's attempt to ridicule England's involvement in the War of Spanish Succession; a sort of eighteenth century *Spitting Image*. For some reason the English didn't really get the joke, instead taking the character to their hearts.

MUIRHEAD GETS THE MESSAGE

Alexander Muirhead was an electrical engineer from East Saltoun, East Lothian, who radically advanced wireless telegraphy. He studied science at St Bartholomew's Hospital in London, where he became the first man to make a recording of a human heartbeat. Muirhead went on to make his name designing precision instruments, and with Herbert Taylor patented 'duplexing' (today in 1878), which first made it possible to send messages through a long ocean cable both ways simultaneously, hugely increasing the speed of global communication.

COOLEST COWS

Cows don't come much harder than Highland Cattle. With their wide, sweeping horns and flowing hair they are clearly the rock stars of the bovine world, and were developed to thrive in conditions where other cattle would wuss out. The Highland Cattle Society was formed today in 1884 to promote the breed. They can now be found looking shaggy and awesome all over the world, and have even been spotted munching meagre grass 10,000ft up in the Andes.

DUNDEE'S BRIGHT SPARK

James Bowman Lindsay of Dundee produced continuous electric light before witnesses at the Thistle Hall today in 1835. This was 45 years before Edison produced his incandescent lamp. Lindsay stated that he could 'read a book at a distance of one and a half feet'. However, the book clearly wasn't one about patent law as Lindsay neither registered nor developed his invention, and so is now largely unknown. His next great advance was translating The Lord's Prayer into 50 languages.

NAPIER GETS THE POINT

Today in 1614 John Napier, an Edinburgh aristocrat, announced he'd discovered logarithms. Most people thought he'd just taken up African drumming, but scientists realised he'd perfected a new method of computation. Using logarithms they could now multiply large numbers in a tenth of the time it used to take, which was still about a week. They look hard work now, but then Napier's advance was as revolutionary as the computer in the twentieth century. For an encore, he introduced the decimal point to mathematics.

THE AULD LASSIE O' THREADNEEDLE STREET

In 1694 England was broke. Then a Scot, William Paterson, proposed a loan of £1.2m to the government in return for which the loan subscribers would be incorporated as 'The Governor and Company of the Bank of England' with banking privileges including the issue of notes. The new bank raised £1.2m in 12 days; half of it used to quadruple England's navy. After England and Scotland were united in 1707, the power of the Navy made Britain the dominant world power in the late eighteenth and early nineteenth centuries.

LAUDER ALMIGHTY

Harry Lauder began singing to relieve the tedium of his coal-mining job. By 1911 he was commanding $1,000 a night in the US and in 1912 he was top of the bill at Britain's first Royal Command Variety performance. Ultimately, Sir Harry Lauder became the first British artiste to sell a million records and was the highest-paid performer in the world, making the equivalent of £12,700 a night plus expenses. Today in 1927 he received the Freedom of his home city of Edinburgh.

STIRLING'S CROWNING GLORY

Perched in a magnificent spot atop the city's highest hill, the Church of the Holy Rude would be a truly famous landmark were it not right next to an even more awesome building, Stirling Castle. The church, founded in 1129, is still the second oldest building in the city and is of huge historical importance. Today in 1567 James VI, the infant son of Mary, Queen of Scots, was crowned there. That makes it the only surviving church in the UK apart from Westminster Abbey to have held a coronation.

BROWN TAKES A CLOSER LOOK

A Scot didn't invent the microscope, but Robert Brown from Montrose made amazing advances in the instrument's use. Brown was a botanist who coined the word 'nucleus' for cells. He named thousands of new plant species and today in 1828 he described the random movement of pollen grains being bombarded by atoms that bears his name – Brownian Motion. This phenomenon is also widely known as 'the-experiment-from-school-that-wasn't-as-much-fun-as-exploding-magnesium'.

LAUNCH OF THE HEBRIDEAN ROCKET POST

Gerhard Zucker was a German rocket engineer who, today in 1934, tried to convince the General Post Office that postal delivery by rocket was viable. He packed his 3ft-long rocket with 1,200 envelopes and a hefty charge of powder, and tried to shoot it over the mile of sea between the islands of Harris and Scarp. Unfortunately the rocket exploded, blowing 'rocket mail' both out of the water and into the water at the same time.

AUGUST

SCOTT'S STARSHIP

1

It might look like a gothic rocket ship, but the Scott Monument (completed today in 1844) on Edinburgh's Princes Street is actually the world's largest monument to a writer. Sir Walter Scott might be little read nowadays but in his lifetime he was a writing rock star of Rowling proportions. The monument to him stands an incredible 200ft 6in high and was designed by George Meikle Kemp, a joiner who taught himself architecture.

AN INDEPENDENT THINKER

John Witherspoon from Gifford in East Lothian was the only clergyman to sign the US Declaration of Independence, today in 1776 (it had been adopted on 4 July, which is now Independence Day, but the official signing was delayed). He rose to prominence as head professor of the tiny Presbyterian College of New Jersey, which trained ministers. Witherspoon remodelled the syllabus on the University of Edinburgh's, added 300 of his own books to the library, and made entrance requirements stiffer. In doing so he turned it into one of the world's premier universities – Princeton. One of his descendants is actress Reese Witherspoon.

LOVE OF LABOUR

Keir Hardie started work at the age of seven, so it's not surprising he became an advocate for workers' rights. He led miners' unions in Lanarkshire before taking his seat today in 1892 as Independent Labour MP for West Ham South. In the following years he helped found the organisation that became the Labour Party. Hardie's policies were considered outrageous by most other MPs at the time, as he stood for such dangerously radical notions as free schooling, pensions and women's right to vote.

GRAND DESIGNS

Edinburgh's grand New Town owes a lot to William Henry Playfair, the great nineteenth century architect, and nephew of the notorious William (see 14 July). His landmarks include Royal and Regent terraces, Donaldson's College for the deaf and New College on the Mound. He also polished off Robert Adam's design for Edinburgh University and co-designed 'Edinburgh's disgrace', the picturesque but half-built replica of the Parthenon on Calton Hill. His finest works are probably the neo-classical buildings of the National Gallery of Scotland and the Royal Scottish Academy, which were finally joined by an underground link, The Playfair Project, today in 2004.

MESSING ABOUT IN BOATS

The Wind In the Willows has been a classic children's tale almost since it was published. The adventures of Mole, Rat, Badger and, of course, Toad of Toad Hall, take place in an idyllic river valley and could hardly be more English. But its author, Kenneth Grahame, was actually born in Edinburgh. Curiously, the title of Chapter 7 was used by Pink Floyd as the title of their first album, *The Piper at the Gates of Dawn*, which was released today in 1967.

CHALMERS IS LICKED

History says that the first postage stamp, the Penny Black, appeared in 1840 courtesy of Englishman Rowland Hill. But James Chalmers, an Arbroath bookseller, wrote an essay proposing an adhesive postage stamp and cancelling device, complete with illustrations of one penny and two-pence values, and sent it to the General Post Office today in 1834. However, since he didn't have a stamp to put on the envelope, it seems they mislaid it and he missed his place in history.

HELMETED HERO

7

Sir Chris Hoy became Britain's most decorated Olympian of all time today in 2012 when he grabbed his sixth gold medal. His stunning ride in the men's keirin meant Britain won seven of the ten track cycling races at London 2012. Hoy is also the most successful Olympic cyclist of all time. He took up cycling aged six, after watching the film *E.T.* with its famous flying bike scene. Out of this world indeed...

COMING TOGETHER

Capturing the summer vibe of the Swinging Sixties and depicting the Beatles just before they broke up, the cover of *Abbey Road* is probably one of the most iconic photos of all time. It was snapped today in 1969 by Scottish photographer Iain Macmillan. To capture the shot, Iain had to perch atop a 10ft stepladder in the middle of the road with a policeman holding back traffic. He got the perfect shot on the fifth snap.

TATTOO HULLABALOO

The Royal Edinburgh Military Tattoo began life today in 1950 as the Army's contribution to the recently established Edinburgh Festival. With just eight items on the programme it drew a few thousand spectators on benches set up on the castle esplanade. Now it's one of the world's most spectacular shows (as long as you find the basic idea of soldiers marching up and down interesting, that is) and is seen by 217,000 people each year and televised to 100 million more worldwide. But, most amazingly considering Scottish summers, a tattoo performance has never been cancelled.

TOP OF THE CHARTS

Before this day in 1795 ship's captains were obliged to source their own navigational charts. As you can imagine, this wasn't the safest state of affairs. Then a Scot, Alexander Dalrymple, became the British Admiralty's first appointed hydrographer. He pointed out that accurate map-making was something the Navy really ought to be doing itself. Thanks to him, by 1884 nearly three-quarters of the world's marine trade relied on maps using British co-ordinates.

MORE, BEARDMORE, MORE

William Beardmore & Co was a giant Glasgow engineering company that made vast numbers of the things that got the world moving – planes, trains, automobiles, motorbikes, even airships. At its peak it employed 40,000 people. Owner William Beardmore also sponsored Ernest Shackleton's first Antarctic expedition, which sailed today in 1907. Shackleton made the first ascent of Mount Erebus, trekked further south than any man before had done, and discovered the world's largest glacier (100 miles long), which he generously named the Beardmore Glacier after his backer.

THE SUPER-CINEMA

The curtain first went up in the Edinburgh Playhouse today in 1929, the largest and most opulent cinema ever built in Scotland that still survives. Designed as a 'super-cinema' that could also house variety shows, it has 3,059 seats, a huge stage and 30 dressing rooms. It is now the UK's largest working theatre and is reputed to have a resident ghost, Albert.

HEROIC ACHIEVEMENTS

Perth-born John Buchan was one of those people who are so amazing at everything it's actually annoying. A published author while still at university, he was president of the Oxford Union and a prize-winning poet and essayist. After careers as a lawyer, diplomat and historian, he settled on writing, and today in 1915 published his most famous book, *The Thirty-Nine Steps*. The thriller was hugely popular as a book and film, and helped create the dashing hero-on-the-run genre of stories. Buchan also became an MP and the Governor-General of Canada. See what I mean?

THE MAD ANATOMIST

John Hunter from East Kilbride was a brilliant but eccentric surgeon who first explained the function of the lymph glands and the structure of the placenta. Hunter developed the standard treatment for a torn tendon, once operating on himself after damaging his own tendon dancing. He also deliberately infected himself with gonorrhoea and syphilis in the name of research. When he moved to a spacious house in Earl's Court he kept a menagerie including a zebra, buffalo and jackals in its grounds, the animals living in apparent peace together. This inspired the character of Doctor Dolittle who first appeared in print, courtesy of author Hugh Lofting, today in 1920.

WAVE POWER

With sea on three sides and what can best be described as 'boisterous' weather, it's no wonder that Scotland is leading the world in wave energy. The Pelamis Wave Energy Converter is an impressive machine made up of connected tubular sections that flex and bend as waves pass to generate electricity. A bit like a giant string of link sausages. Built in Leith, it became the world's first offshore wave machine to generate electricity when it was connected to the UK grid today in 2004. Next stop, solar power from square sausage...

GIVE ME A WAVE

You might think a nineteenth century naval engineer and fibre optic cables have little in common. But John Scott Russell was walking along the Union Canal in Edinburgh today in 1834 when he saw a boat create a peculiar standing wave that moved without losing speed or height. Little was done with what is now known as a 'soliton' until its properties proved perfect for high-speed TV, telephone and computer connections. A fibre-optic cable linking Edinburgh and Glasgow now runs beneath the same towpath on which Russell stood 160 years ago – and you thought *you* had to wait a long time for your broadband to be installed!

THE KILT RISES IN POPULARITY

When Highland dress was banned in 1746 after the second Jacobite uprising it became a romantic symbol of an oppressed people. But although the ban was lifted in 1782, the kilt wasn't properly revived until writer Sir Walter Scott stage-managed the visit of King George IV to Edinburgh today in 1822. In keeping with his romantic take on Scottish history Scott had the King and most of the crowd wear a kilt. The draughty garment made a swirling comeback.

A VERSE TO WAR

18

A rambling, half-ruined psychiatric hospital on a dark, wooded hill outside Edinburgh is perhaps an odd place for one of twentieth century literature's great encounters. But that is exactly what happened when Siegfried Sassoon and Wilfred Owen, soldier poets and passionate critics of the Great War, met at Craiglockhart War Hospital today in 1917. Owen, who died the following year, was transformed as a poet by the encounter and soon wrote many of his most famous pieces, including 'Dulce et Decorum Est'.

THE KEYS TO SUCCESS

John Broadwood & Sons is the name on some of the oldest and finest pianos in the world, and their instruments have been played by Mozart, Haydn, Chopin, Beethoven and Liszt. Broadwood himself was a Scottish carpenter who walked the 400 miles from his village of Oldhamstocks to London in 1761 to seek his fortune. He worked for a Swiss harpsichord manufacturer before taking over the company that bears his name today in 1773. Later he helped perfect the modern grand piano.

EXPLOSIVE THINKING

Your picnic tea stays piping hot thanks to cool thinking from Scottish physicist Sir James Dewar, who invented the vacuum flask in 1892. Alas, he neglected to patent it and two German glass-blowers registered the trademark 'Thermos'. He did, however, remember to patent another of his creations – cordite (today in 1890), which totally replaced gunpowder in British military firearms.

IT'S WRITTEN IN THE STARS – WELL, THE *EXPRESS*

John Gordon was a Dundee-born journalist who rose to become editor of the *Sunday Express*. He published Britain's first newspaper crossword and, when he was looking for a novel way to celebrate the birth of Princess Margaret today in 1930, he commissioned the first newspaper horoscope. The mixture of predictions and random gibberish was wildly popular and it became a regular feature. Its author, R.H. Naylor, now needed a simple way of producing regular daily predictions, so he created the zodiac sun-sign system of astrology.

RIDING OUT FOR REVELRY

Most of the men of Hawick were felled at the disastrous Battle of Flodden in 1513. On this day the next year, several young lads, or 'callants', fought and famously defeated a section of Lord Dacre's English army, capturing its flag. Their fighting spirit is commemorated every summer in the Common-Ridings at Hawick and other Border towns. A 'Cornet' is elected as figurehead for a week of races, parades, ride-outs to surrounding villages – and drinking on an historic scale, of course.

FRINGE BENEFITS

'The best of the world's performing arts' – that's what the Edinburgh International Festival aimed to celebrate when it first got under way today in 1947. But the event was quickly gate-crashed by unofficial performers who created the much edgier 'Fringe'. Now the world's largest cultural event, this hosts over 2,500 international shows from 60 nations in 258 venues annually, and launched stars including Alan Bennett, Dudley Moore, Peter Cook, Tom Stoppard and Derek Jacobi. Despite all the mainstream success, the average Fringe audience still numbers only nine people.

DEEP-FRIED TROUBLE FOR OUR ARTERIES

Originally, the deep-fried Mars Bar was a bit of fun between the owner of the Haven Chip Bar (now the Carron) in Stonehaven and some local kids. But when the *Daily Record* ran an article on it today in 1995, the idea – and myth – soon spread to the national press, TV and the BBC World Service. Even though we didn't really eat them, people thought it highly likely that we *would*, and so it became a self-fulfilling prophecy. Now a quarter of all Scottish chippies serve them. Which says a lot, really.

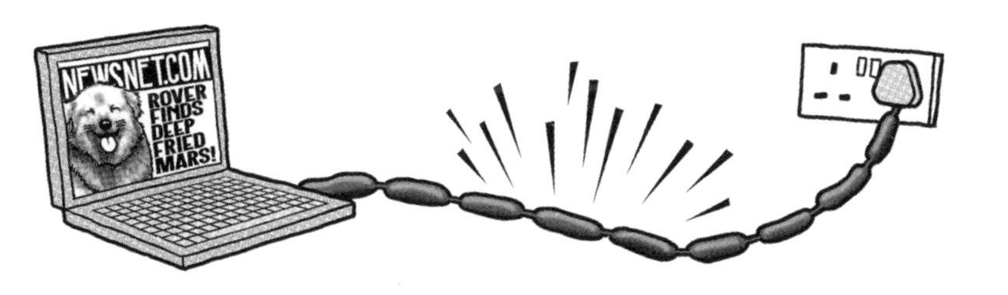

CARNEGIE, KING OF THE LIBRARIES

Andrew Carnegie left Scotland as a poor weaver's son and in America became one of the richest men who has ever lived (today his fortune would be worth $300 billion; Bill Gates's stash is just $40 billion). He wanted to put self-improvement in the hands of everyone, and today in 1883 he opened a free public library in his home town of Dunfermline. Carnegie went on to fund, build and stock an incredible 2,500 public libraries in the UK and US.

PART MAN, PART MACHINE, ALL SCOTTISH

We can rebuild him ... no, not Steve Austin, the original Six Million Dollar Man, but a hotelier called Campbell Aird who today in 1998 became the first man in the world to have a bionic arm. The electronic limb was a major advance in prosthetics, and was developed by a team at Edinburgh's Princess Margaret Rose Orthopaedic Hospital. Aird was a determined fellow – after losing his arm to cancer in 1982 he managed to windsurf one-armed across the English Channel and won 14 trophies for clay-pigeon shooting. After his operation he won an appearance in the *Guinness Book of Records* as the 'man with the most successful false arm'.

TYTLER TAKES OFF

James Tytler from Angus was a 'lad o' pairts' whose career included surgeon, chemist, printer, poet, journalist, professional revolutionary and editor of the *Encyclopaedia Britannica*. None of these proved profitable so, inspired as much by a need to drum up some cash to feed his five children as he was by the recent exploits of the Montgolfier brothers, he designed and built his own hot-air balloon. Today in 1784 he successfully flew it to a height of 350ft above Edinburgh and so became Britain's first aeronaut.

A MAGNETIC PERSONALITY

Professor John Mallard was the head of medical physics at Aberdeen University for 27 years, where he led the team that helped develop the MRI (Magnetic Resonance Imaging) body-scanning machine. They first used it on a patient from Fraserburgh, Aberdeenshire, today in 1980, since when it has helped millions of patients worldwide. In many ways, MRI has been as important to medicine as the discovery of X-rays was in 1895. Mind you, it's a good job they don't use MRI scanners at airports or we'd never had time to hit the duty free!

RAEBURN'S RARE TALENT

Henry Raeburn was a poor orphan who showed enough artistic skill to become an apprentice goldsmith. His master nurtured Henry's talent and the lad went on to become one of Scotland's greatest artists. He painted portraits of the big names in the Scottish Enlightenment, from James Hutton to Sir Walter Scott, and was knighted by George IV today in 1822. His 'Skating Minister' is one of the country's favourite pictures and an icon of Scottish culture.

WET AND WILD

It's not just Scotland's weather that is impressively grumpy, we can be proud of our fearsome waters too. The Corryvreckan whirlpool, off Jura's northern tip, is one of the largest in the world. Flood tides can power waves 30ft high, and the roar of the maelstrom can be heard 10 miles away. Corryvreckan made the news today in 1947 when author George Orwell (who was then writing *1984* on Jura) nearly got himself and his companions drowned by steering their rowing boat into the whirlpool.

FEELING CHIPPER

'Silicon Glen' might have started as a self-deprecating joke, but it became an economic wonder. Success started today in 1960 when Hughes Aircraft opened its first facility outside the US in Glenrothes, making silicon diodes. A wave of other technology manufacturers followed, setting up home across central Scotland from Ayrshire to Dundee. At its peak the area had one of the greatest concentrations of high-tech industry in the world, and produced 30 per cent of Europe's PCs, 65 per cent of its ATMs and a huge percentage of its integrated circuits.

SEPTEMBER

POSTCARDS GET IN THE PICTURE

Today in 1894, the Post Office ruled that privately printed picture postcards could be mailed as long as they had a halfpenny stamp. One of the first publishers to add pictures to cards was George Stewart of 92 George Street, Edinburgh. Holidaying families have been happily buying postcards and then forgetting to send them until they get home ever since.

FLIGHT OF FANCY

2

One of the world's earliest serious attempts at human flight happened in the unlikely environs of Stirling Castle today in 1507. John Damian, an alchemist, surgeon and all-round nutjob at the court of James IV, built himself some wings, glued feathers all over them and proclaimed that he would fly to France. Given that the castle stands atop a 250ft sheer rock, you have to admire his commitment. However, he failed completely, landing in a dunghill and breaking his thigh.

FLEMING'S MIRACULOUS MIDDEN

200 million lives saved, all thanks to a Scottish slob. Scientist Alexander Fleming couldn't be bothered tidying up his lab when he went on holiday and when he returned today in 1928 there were contaminated bacteria cultures all over his workbench. But Fleming was amazed to see that a fungus had killed patches of bacteria on the clarty dishes. He developed that fungus into penicillin, the single greatest life-saving drug the world has seen. It would conquer syphilis, gangrene, tuberculosis and many other infections.

THE ORIGINAL TARTAN ARMY

The Atholl Highlanders are the only remaining private army in Europe. They were originally formed as a ceremonial bodyguard for Lord Glenlyon, later 6th Duke of Atholl. But Queen Victoria was impressed with them on her first visit to Scotland in 1842, and made them her Guards of Honour. She granted them colours and thus the right to bear arms today in 1845.

FLYING AHEAD OF HIS TIME

5

Naval architect Percy Pilcher was a student of Lord Kelvin at Glasgow University and, very nearly, the first man to demonstrate powered flight. In 1897, Pilcher built a hang-glider called 'The Hawk' with which he broke the world distance record by flying 820ft. He also designed a powered triplane but days before he was due to fly it, he crashed his glider and died. A reconstruction today in 2003 proved his design would have flown, and beaten the Wright brothers into the air by four years.

STIRLING CASTLE TOPS THE LOT

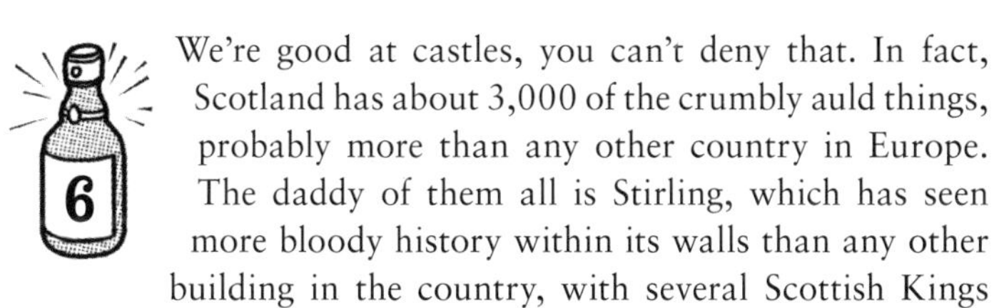

We're good at castles, you can't deny that. In fact, Scotland has about 3,000 of the crumbly auld things, probably more than any other country in Europe. The daddy of them all is Stirling, which has seen more bloody history within its walls than any other building in the country, with several Scottish Kings and Queens crowned there, including Mary, Queen of Scots. Today in 2012 it proved its mettle yet again, beating the Tower of London and the Houses of Parliament to be rated Britain's top tourist spot.

I'M GINGER AND I'M PROUD

The first-ever Redhead Day happened today in 2005 when the Dutch painter Bart Rouwenhorst gathered lots of russet-haired lasses together. He claims he was inspired by artists like Dante Gabriel Rossetti and Gustav Klimt, but really he just loves gingers. Which makes him all right by us. After all, we have the world's highest proportion of redheads – 13 per cent of the population, compared with 4 per cent for Europe as a whole. Incidentally, gingers need more anaesthetic than dull-headed folk, which is maybe why we drink so much booze.

PAWNED BUT NEVER REDEEMED

We Scots can be proud of a particularly smooth bit of business by King James III today in 1468. When he agreed to marry Margaret, daughter of King Christian I of Norway, he demanded a dowry of 60,000 florins. Like many fathers of the bride, Christian was a bit short at the time and so canny King James suggested taking Orkney and Shetland as security until he could stump up the cash. Christian never did, so the islands have been ours ever since.

TOP TOUN

Say 'skyscrapers' and you probably think 'New York'. But back in the seventeenth century it was Edinburgh that had the world's true High Street. Thanks to the Battle of Flodden (today in 1513) we got paranoid about the English (funny, that) and constructed a massive wall around the capital. The only place to build extra space was up, and soon buildings of 11 storeys were common, with a few tenements topping 14 and even 15 floors. Many are still inhabited today, mostly by English students...

GAME, SET AND MATCH, MURRAY!

Andy Murray went where Tim Henman (and 76 years' worth of other male British tennis players) had failed to go when he won a major tennis tournament today in 2012. Hailing from Glasgow (and proud!), Murray triumphed in the US Open, beating Serbian Novak Djokovic in an epic match. With this 'major' under his belt, plus a Gold Olympic medal at London 2012, many commentators believe there's now nothing he cannot achieve. Let's hope that includes a decent haircut.

TO BE OR NOT TO BE ... NAKED

Hamlet doesn't normally get parties of schoolkids on their feet and cheering, but then not every theatre plays it like the Citizens in Glasgow – with oodles of nudity. The theatre's refreshing approach to drama has included an equally saucy *Dracula* (a sellout), reasonable ticket prices and its own children's company. Originally opened today in 1878, the Citizens has an extremely impressive list of alumni. Thesps who have trod its boards include: Tim Roth, Gary Oldman, Alan Rickman, Sean Bean, Robbie Coltrane, Tim Curry, Robert Carlyle and Pierce Brosnan. Not all of them appeared nude, though.

STOP INTERFERON WITH YOURSELF

Alick Isaacs was a virologist from Glasgow who identified the first interferon, a protein that helps trigger the body's immune system. He published his results today in 1957 with Swiss researcher Jean Lindenmann, and their findings led to important new treatments for a range of viruses, bacterial infections and cancers. Interferons are also very useful in combating genital warts, which is surely something to be proud of.

NO, THERE ISN'T AN IN-FLIGHT MOVIE

The world's shortest scheduled airline flight is a 1.7-mile hop between the islands Westray and Papa Westray in Orkney – about the length of the main runway at Edinburgh Airport. You reach the plane not via a departure lounge but through a field gate that serves as a customs barrier. The Loganair service, inaugurated today in 1967, lasts just two minutes, but the record with a favourable wind is 58 seconds. Loganair also fly to the only airstrip that is open 'subject to tides' – Barra's runway is a beach.

BROADSWORD CALLING DANNY BOY

If you love curling up on a winter sofa to watch a rattling good war movie, you owe a big 'thank you' to Alistair MacLean. Born in Glasgow, MacLean used his real-life war experiences to write a series of cracking thrillers, many of which became classic films. His first novel, *HMS Ulysses*, was published today in 1955 and became instantly popular, and he went on to write *The Guns of Navarone*, *Ice Station Zebra* and *Where Eagles Dare*. Not bad considering English was his second language – he was originally brought up speaking Gaelic.

THAT'S NOT A HOT DOG

Green's Playhouse in Glasgow was the largest cinema in Europe when it opened today in 1927, seating 4,368 people. It was demolished in 1987 and the site is now occupied by the Cineworld Renfrew Street, the world's tallest cinema at 203ft high. Landmark though this is, it lacks the Playhouse's famous 'double divan' seats, which were, for some reason, extraordinarily popular with courting couples.

TALKIN' HEIDS

The American new-wave band Talking Heads was one of the most influential (and tuneful) bands of its time. They released their first single today in 1977 and went on to record a string of acclaimed songs, including 'Road To Nowhere' and 'Burning Down The House'. The band's lead singer David Byrne has earned Grammy, Oscar and Golden Globe awards and been inducted to the Rock and Roll Hall of Fame. He was also born in Dumbarton.

BIGGEST WEE COUNTRY IN THE WORLD

Deep in the Borders near Eddleston is the world's largest terrain relief model – The Great Polish Map of Scotland. Built by Polish nationals in recognition of Scottish hospitality during the Second World War, this giant three-dimensional map sits in an oval pool 160ft wide and 5ft deep and once flowed with water, recreating rivers, lochs and seas. The map secured listed status today in 2012, kick-starting a restoration project to give it a much-needed clean and 'polish'.

HEAD IN THE CLOUDS

Standing in the rain on top of Ben Nevis, most of us would have our hoods up and our heads down, but today in 1894 physicist Charles T.R. Wilson was gazing up in wonder at the dreich sky. He was entranced by the way light shining on droplets of the mist around him formed beautiful shapes and coronas, and he used these observations to invent the cloud chamber in 1911. This allowed the paths of subatomic particles to be seen for the first time, giving a massive boost to atomic physics and winning him the Nobel Prize.

ARMADA HERE

Ask any English schoolboy and he'll tell you that Sir Francis Drake's triumph over the Spanish Armada was one of England's great naval victories. But that battle more scattered than vanquished the enemy fleet. It was when the Spaniards first rounded Cape Wrath today in 1588 that they really hit trouble. Our lovely summer weather performed its usual tricks and dozens of ships were smashed onto our west coast, never to trouble England again. So we're due a wee bit of thanks.

ROSSLYN'S ROAMER

Rosslyn Chapel is one of the most beautiful and mysterious buildings in the world – it has glorious architecture, exquisite carvings and, apparently, is where Tom Hanks nearly found the Holy Grail. Even cooler is the secret hidden in its decorations. Construction began today in 1456, 50 years before Columbus even set sail for the New World, yet many carvings appear to show ears of American maize. To many this is glorious proof that a Scotsman, Henry Sinclair, Earl of Orkney and grandfather of the chapel's founder, actually discovered America before Columbus.

SCOTLAND IS GROWING PLACES

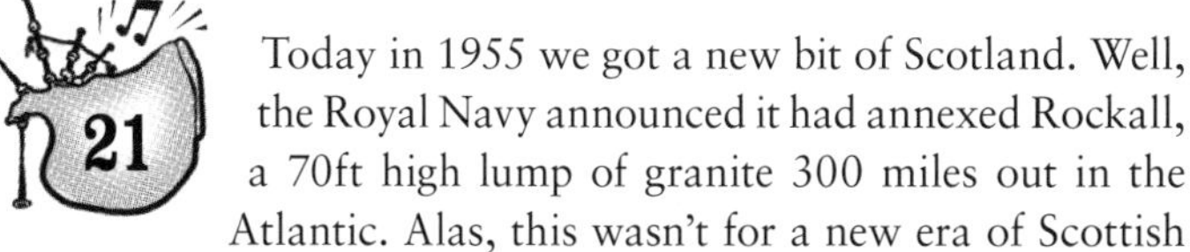

Today in 1955 we got a new bit of Scotland. Well, the Royal Navy announced it had annexed Rockall, a 70ft high lump of granite 300 miles out in the Atlantic. Alas, this wasn't for a new era of Scottish empire building, but because they were worried that Russia might use the rock as an observation post to spy on nearby missile tests. They dropped two marines and a naturalist on it to run a flag up. Fittingly, the commander of the mission was called Scott.

FLOWER POWERED

Aberdeen is famous for its grey granite buildings, and the stone is justly famous. It was used to build the terraces of the Houses of Parliament and Waterloo Bridge in London, while Marischal College on Broad Street is the second largest granite building in the world. (Its source, Rubislaw Quarry, which closed in 1971, is one of the biggest man-made holes in Europe.) But the city is also one of the most colourful in the world – it won the Britain in Bloom competition for a record-breaking tenth time today in 2006.

STEVE STARTS HIS EDUCATION

Today in 2001 a nineteen-year-old lad called Steve started his art history course at St Andrews University. What's so inspiring about that? Well, he met his future wife in his flat-share. Still not impressed? Well, he also enjoyed partying quite a lot. Good, no? Okay, he was also a prince, and the future king of Great Britain and the Commonwealth – 'Steve' was what fellow students called Prince William to prevent earwigging journalists from knowing what he got up to in his four years in Fife.

SUCCESS WENT TO HIS HEID

Ah, the great sights of the world – the majesty of the Taj Mahal, the beauty of the Grand Canyon ... and the daftness of Glasgow's Duke of Wellington statue with a traffic cone on his head. For this student-prank-turned-art-institution isn't just one of the city's iconic images, but was officially named as one of the world's ultimate sights by Lonely Planet, today in 2011.

LAYING A MIGHTY CABLE

The first transatlantic telephone call by submarine cable took place today in 1956, thanks to the TAT-1 (Transatlantic No. 1) cable, which came ashore under the fishing boats in Gallanach Bay, near Oban. At the other end, 3,884 miles away, was Clarenville, Newfoundland. As well as ordinary calls, the cable also carried the famous 'Hot Line' of the Cold War – does that make it 'cool'? – allowing private chats between the world's leaders.

GLENEAGLES MAKES ITS MARK ON SOCIETY

Gleneagles is one of the world's greatest hotels, which made its name as part of the 'high society' calendar. After the London 'season' it was yachting at Cowes, polo at Deauville and golf and grouse shooting at Gleneagles. It hosted the world's most important leaders (and Silvio Berlusconi) at the G8 summit in 2005 and today in 2014 the next Ryder Cup will commence. You might be surprised to learn that *Fawlty Towers* was inspired by the Gleneagles Hotel; a down-at-heel one in Torquay, naturally, not our swish version.

GOING COMMANDO

The Commando Memorial (unveiled today in 1952) near Spean Bridge is one of Britain's best-known war memorials. This huge statue enjoys a stunning mountain location and pays tribute to the elite force formed in 1940. The Commando Training Centre was nearby, and prospective Commandos had to speed-march the seven miles from the station to the centre with full kit and weapon (weighing 36lb). Anyone not arriving within 60 minutes immediately failed selection, which is a pretty tough first day on the job.

YOU'VE GOT TO FLING IT TO WIN IT

Easdale Quarry in Argyll produced slate so beautiful that it was exported all over the British Empire. It also makes for world-class skimming stones and since this day in 1997, the World Stone Skimming Championships have taken place here. Scotland's own Dougie Isaacs has won an incredible four times, giving us a genuine world champion. The fact that Easdale is pretty hard for overseas competitors to get to is irrelevant.

SCOTLAND'S SOUTHERN COPPERS

In the fifteenth and sixteenth centuries, Scottish diplomats visiting English royalty in London would stay in a little corner of Westminster near what is now Whitehall. Over time this became a site of government buildings and residences for civil servants. When the Metropolitan Police was formed by Sir Robert Peel today in 1829, the new force made its base in 4 Whitehall Place. This backed on to a street that still bore the name Great Scotland Yard, which is why London's Metropolitan Police Service headquarters is known as Scotland Yard.

THE KING OF CONSERVATION

Yosemite Valley in the US is one of the world's most stunning natural wonders. That it isn't one vast sheep farm is down to John Muir from Dunbar. Muir's family left for the wilds of Wisconsin when he was eleven and he grew up bonkers for all things botanical. A conservation pioneer, he was the founder of the US National Park system, which came into being today in 1890 and now protects an area almost three times the size of Scotland.

OCTOBER

IRON-WILLED

In the early nineteenth century ironmasters were convinced that cold air was best used in their blast furnaces. James Neilson, a manager of a gasworks from Shettleston, disagreed and developed a new 'hot blast' technique (patented today in 1828). He was spectacularly right – his method tripled the quantity of iron that could be produced from a given amount of fuel and allowed raw coal rather than coke to be used. By 1860, 90 per cent of Britain's iron was made by hot blast and Neilson's innovation led to the stratospheric growth of the Scottish iron industry. So it's not always bad to be full of hot air...

TV IS A REALITY

John Logie Baird from Helensburgh made the first television transmission of a moving image today in 1925. This being the days before any old numpty would throw themselves in front of a camera, he had to bribe a terrified office boy, William Taynton, to be the first person to appear on TV. Audiences had to wait 55 years, though, for the next great televisual advance from Scotland – *Take the High Road*.

PLASTIC FANTASTIC

Aberfeldy Golf Club needed a new bridge over the River Tay, but couldn't afford a metal one, so they asked engineering students from Dundee to design and build an alternative. The students surpassed themselves, finding the energy to complete it during the summer vacation and using plastic as a building material. It opened today in 1993, and at over 300ft long it is the longest plastic bridge in the world. Amazing what you can do with old Pot Noodle containers, isn't it?

BET HIS MILEAGE IS PISH, THOUGH

Today in 1983, Richard Noble from Edinburgh set a world land speed record of 1,019km/h (633.468mph) in his *Thrust2* turbojet car. No, he wasn't fleeing from the polis on the bypass, he was in the Black Rock Desert, Nevada. Noble was also director of the project that smashed this record in 1997, *ThrustSSC*. This car, driven by Andy Green, went supersonic, reaching 1,228km/h (763.035mph) .

SHAKEN, NOT SHTIRRED...

It all started today in 1961 for Big Tam from Fountainbridge – sorry, Sir Sean Connery. The thirty-one-year-old actor was announced as the star of the first James Bond film. Author Ian Fleming initially didn't think much of Connery, calling him 'an overgrown stunt-man'. But he warmed to his performance and gave Bond Scottish ancestry in subsequent novels. Connery, of course, went on to become one of the biggest movie stars of all time.

DESIGN TO A TEA

Charles Rennie Mackintosh was an architect, designer and artist whose unique stylings captivated the Art Nouveau movement. He designed Glasgow School of Art, the Glasgow Herald building and Mackintosh House, and had a considerable influence on European design. His famous Willow Tearooms on Sauchiehall Street have been selling scones to old ladies in large purple hats since this day in 1903.

FERGUSON FIRES FIRST

Muzzle-loading eighteenth century muskets were pretty good at killing people, but then Captain Patrick Ferguson of Pitfours came up with the brilliant idea of the breech-loading rifle. It was used in the American War of Independence at the Battle of Saratoga today in 1777 and proved far more efficient. A skilled rifleman could now blow holes in people 10 times per minute. Another proud Scottish achievement!

TOP ATTRACTION

At 417ft high, the Tower at Glasgow Science Centre is the tallest tower in Scotland and the tallest structure in the world that can wholly revolve through 360 degrees. Visitors first enjoyed its breathtaking views today in 2001. Designed as an aerofoil, it moves with the wind but, thankfully, its rotation is computer-controlled: if it could spin on its own with our weather they'd never get the damn thing stopped.

HE'S HAD HIS OATS

Considering we invented the stuff, it's only fair that one of our boys won the World Porridge-Making Championships at Carrbridge, today in 2011. John Boa, a Gaelic singer from Edinburgh, picked up the highly prized Golden Spurtle, fighting off rivals from as far off as California. Incidentally, porridge is so good for energy that Usain Bolt clearly modelled his victory pose on the shotputter on the Scott's Porage Oat boxes...

BROUGHAM'S CANNES-DO ATTITUDE

Some people really do get things done. Henry Brougham was a successful lawyer and statesman, who became Lord Chancellor. Brougham co-founded the influential *Edinburgh Review* (today in 1802) and helped pass the Slavery Abolition Act. He designed the brougham carriage that bears his name and when he bought land in the then tiny French fishing village of Cannes, he turned it into a fashionable resort. A man of words as well as action, he still holds the House of Commons record for nonstop speaking at six hours.

BRAINY BEASTIE

American researchers had the temerity to try and prove the existence of the Loch Ness Monster today in 1987. They used 24 boats and the latest sonar technology to make the biggest sweep of any freshwater lake in the world. Nessie, of course, did exactly what you'd expect in the face of such an unwelcome overseas intrusion: kept a low profile. The canny beastie made just enough of a blip on the sonar to keep the tourist dollars coming but refrained from causing a scene.

A SWIMMINGLY GOOD CAREER

Sir Robert Matthew was a brilliant Scottish modernist architect who designed the Royal Festival Hall in London (Clement Attlee laid the foundation stone today in 1949). He co-founded the famous RMJM architecture firm, designed New Zealand House in London and Pakistan's new capital buildings in Islamabad. Best of all, though, he designed the Royal Commonwealth Pool – the legendary 'Commie' – in Edinburgh.

THE MAGIC OF MARMALADE

Janet Keiller's husband James was a Dundee merchant who bought a duff shipload of oranges in 1797. Forced to do something to get his money back, his wife made an almighty batch of marmalade. This turned out nicely and soon the Keillers had founded the world's very first marmalade factory. One of their biggest fans is undoubtedly Paddington Bear, who first appeared today in 1958, courtesy of Scottish publishers William Collins & Sons.

THE FIRST SURVIVOR

Fife-born sailor Alexander Selkirk doubted the seaworthiness of the ship he was sailing on and begged to be set ashore. Alas, the island he chose, Juan Fernández off the coast of Chile, was uninhabited. Selkirk spent the next four years and four months utterly alone, eating goats and wild turnips. He was finally rescued and returned to Britain today in 1711, becoming the inspiration for Daniel Defoe's famous *Robinson Crusoe*, the original survival story.

HOLLOW MOUNTAIN

A kilometre inside Ben Cruachan is the world's first reversible pump storage hydro system (which opened today in 1965). It functions as a power station and a vast storage battery: water rushes down tunnels from a dam high in the hills above to power turbines, and can also be pumped up from the loch below in quiet times, ready to be used when 5 million kettles get flicked on. The turbine hall is hewn out of solid rock and cavernous enough to house the Tower of London.

BATHGATE'S BIGGEST WINNER

Dario Franchitti might be just about the most glamorous thing ever to come out of Bathgate. His name sounds cool to start with, and he is an amazing racing driver, who has won the famous Indianapolis 500 three times and the IndyCar championships four times (achieved today in 2011). His brother Marino is a Le Mans 24-hour driver, while cousin Paul di Resta drives in Formula One – there must be something in the Bathgate water…

PAR FOR THE COURSE

The world's oldest golf tournament in existence, and golf's first major, is the Open Championship, which saw golfers first teeing off today in 1860 at Prestwick Golf Club in Ayrshire. Shortly afterwards, a visiting American became the first person to shout 'Get in the hole!' when someone putted, and was promptly clubbed to death, Scots golfers being a rough bunch in those days. Not any more, though…

BET YOUR HEDGING

Next time you're tootling through rural Perthshire, watch out for the beech hedge near Meikleour – it's the tallest in the world. Planting began today in 1745 and the story goes that the trees grow so high because they are reaching for the heavens, as the men who planted it were killed at the Battle of Culloden the following year. The hedge is now a world-beating 100ft in height and it stretches for a third of a mile along the A93. The only people with ladders long enough to keep it trim are the fire brigade, who get their gardening gloves out once every 10 years.

HIC,HIC, HOORAY!

Edinburgh University students are proud to get drunk at the Teviot in Bristo Square – it's the oldest Student Union building in the world. It opened today in 1889 and presumably the first undergraduate vomited into a potted plant approximately 40 minutes later. The labyrinthine building has eight bars, a nightclub and, apparently, a debating chamber, but no one has bothered to find out where that is.

A TRUE LOCAL HERO

Thirty-four-year-old William Forsyth was getting by making documentary films when he put together a low-budget feature with youth theatre actors and released it today in 1980. Called *That Sinking Feeling*, it didn't exactly set the world on fire, but it did get his next film, *Gregory's Girl*, made. This went a wee bit stratospheric and Bill went on to make more classic Scottish movies that the world also loved, including *Comfort and Joy* and *Local Hero*.

MY ENTRY'S IN THE POST

Glasgow's Burrell Collection is one of the most gloriously barmy art collections in the world, with everything from Chinese porcelain and medieval furniture to paintings by Renoir and Cézanne. Amassed by wealthy ship owner Sir William Burrell, it was donated to the city in 1944. The museum opened to the public today in 1983 and for once we should be glad for a postal strike: if the original deadline for design competition entries hadn't been extended, the winning building would not have been considered.

DARWIN EVOLVES

Sixteen-year-old Charles Darwin enrolled at Edinburgh University to study medicine today in 1825 and fell into an extraordinary intellectual scene. Old College then had one of Europe's finest natural history museums – radical doctor Robert Grant took Darwin sponge collecting and pointed out how humble and advanced animals share similar organs. Darwin learned taxidermy from John Edmonstone, a freed black slave, and met the famous bird illustrator Audubon. He also published his first scientific paper at the city's Plinian Society. Ultimately, though, we can be proud of one particular achievement – Darwin detested his actual medical studies here so much that he promptly gave up the subject and turned to botany instead.

ROCK 'N' ROLL 'N' PERTHSHIRE

Sitting square on the Highland Boundary Fault, Comrie is known as the 'Shakey Toun' for its high frequency of earthquakes. Following the Great Earthquake today in 1839, local postmaster Peter Macfarlane and shoemaker James Drummond set up the world's first modern seismometer here. After more tremors hit in 1869, the 'Earthquake House' was built to hold the instruments. Designated as a building of special architectural interest in 1977, it's the smallest listed building in Britain.

GRIZZLY DISCOVERY

Dr John Rae from Orkney was an explorer who found the final navigable link in the much sought-after Northwest Passage (a sea route in the Arctic joining the Atlantic Ocean to the Pacific Ocean). But he is little known in history. His discovery that a previous expedition, led by Sir John Franklin, had resorted to cannibalism did not sit well with Franklin's widow. When he returned and published this (today in 1854), she organised a blizzard of publicity rubbishing his claim and Rae was promptly shunned by the Establishment.

BIRD-BRAINED BOOK IDEA

When naturalist J.J. Audubon decided to paint every bird in America at life-size and publish the paintings in a huge book, he couldn't find an engraver good enough to reproduce his pictures in the US. So he came to Edinburgh, where he met master engraver William Lizars, today in 1826. Lizars engraved some of his plates, agreed to publish his project and had a famous portrait of Audubon painted, which is now in the White House. Today *Birds of America* is the world's most valuable book: a copy sold in 2010 for £7.3 million.

GO WEST

26

The California gold rush didn't work out for John West, who had left Linlithgow for America. So he settled in Oregon and used his millwright skills to build a sawmill. This prospered and he then turned to exporting barrels of salted salmon back to Britain. West invented an automated can-filling machine, which helped him dominate the market, and his products won a gold medal today in 1873. His name lives on today as the John West brand of canned foods and in the town of Westport in Oregon.

BOYS WILL BE BOYS

The Boys' Brigade was founded in Glasgow by Mr W.A. Smith (born today in 1854) to 'develop Christian manliness by the use of a semi-military discipline and order, gymnastics, summer camps and religious services and classes'. Good times. However, one of its early officers was Robert Baden-Powell, who went on to form the Scouts. I wonder where he got the idea from?

FAULDS MAKES AN IMPRESSION

Henry Faulds was an Ayrshire doctor who became a missionary in Japan, founding the first Japanese society for the blind in 1875. He also introduced Lister's antiseptic methods to Japanese surgeons and halted a rabies epidemic. On what must have been a rare day off Foulds attended an archaeological dig and noticed how finger impressions were left in old clay. He theorised that individual prints were unique and today in 1880 he published a paper in the journal *Nature*, 'On the Skin-furrows of the Hand', which is one of the earliest works on the science of fingerprinting.

HUG-A-SHEEP DAY

It's National Hug-a-sheep Day, and the only reason you can even contemplate such an activity is thanks to George Wilson of Coldstream, who invented the world's first sheep dip in 1830. Before that, sheep were all absolutely louping with various ticks, mites, larvae and lice. Wilson's dip was based on arsenic powder, which certainly sorted the parasites out, even if it wasn't so great for the farmers. Or the sheep either, come to think of it. Anyway, happy hugging!

I WILL WALK 500 MILES (NEARLY)

Meandering for 470 miles through some of Scotland's most beautiful and rugged landscapes, the Scottish National Trail is a long-distance walking route that compares with the best in the world. The longest walking route in the country, the trail was officially opened today in 2012. Running from Yetholm in the Borders to Cape Wrath, the most northwestern point on the British mainland, it means that proud walkers can now be bitten by midges in every corner of the country.

SAMHAIN

With Halloween seeming so Americanised now, you can be proud that Scotland has long had its own distinctive tradition on this day. Samhain ('sow-un') is the Celtic festival celebrating the start of winter. Spirits of the dead abound on this night and so the traditions of guising (to fool the spirits), lantern carving and playing pranks began. And trick-or-treating came from the practice of collecting food for Samhain feasts. So Halloween has actually become more Scottish over the years!

NOVEMBER

POSTIE'S FAVOURITE

Ebenezer Place in Wick isn't famous for being where Scrooge lived – it's actually the shortest street in the world. Just 6ft 9in long, it has only one address: No. 1 Bistro, part of Mackay's Hotel. Built in 1883, its tiny top status was officially recognised today in 2006. Maybe the miserly builders didn't want to spend the money on making it any longer...

PICK UP A PENGUIN

William Speirs Bruce is one of Scotland's greatest, but least-known, explorers. After his studies at Edinburgh University he became an oceanographer and, today in 1902, Bruce sailed from Troon to explore Antarctica. He built the first manned meteorological station there and discovered new land to the east of the Weddell Sea, which he named 'Coats Land' after the Paisley thread-manufacturing family that had backed his expedition. Spears also established the Scottish Ski Club and co-founded Edinburgh Zoo, which he helped stock by helping himself to some penguins on his Antarctic adventures.

THE SEA OF BLACK GOLD

A new energy era dawned today in 1975, when the first oil was pumped from a UK field in the North Sea. The well was in BP's Forties field, 110 miles east of Aberdeen, which was the first and largest oil reserve discovered in the area. With a total reserve of 5 billion barrels of crude oil, its discovery was good news for the British economy, and for luxury car dealerships in the Aberdeen area.

NILE NAVIGATED

James Bruce was a truly remarkable man – he could speak 11 languages and was an accomplished astronomer, historian, geographer, linguist, botanist, ornithologist and cartographer. After several years spent fighting, hunting and debauching his way across Africa, today in 1770 he led his small party to a little swamp with a hillock sticking out of it. This was the fabled source of the Blue Nile, and Bruce was the first to accurately trace it. Unfortunately, his adventures were so extraordinary that no one believed him for years.

I WONDER WHAT THIS ONE DOES-ZZZ

Dr James Young Simpson enjoyed nothing more than having a few friends round and after dinner getting them to inhale various chemicals to determine their medical properties. One night he and his chums tried a new concoction and next thing they knew the sun was streaming in through the window. Simpson had just discovered the anaesthetic effect of chloroform (today in 1847). The medical establishment was sceptical, but he perfected the anaesthetic and when Queen Victoria used it during labour in 1853, a new era of pain-free surgery began.

FERGIE'S FINEST

6

When Alex Ferguson joined Manchester United today in 1986 the once-mighty club hadn't won the League for 20 years. To say Fergie turned them round is an understatement: after a slow start, under his rule they have won 12 League titles, 5 FA Cups and 2 Champions League titles, making him one of the most successful managers in the history of the game. Sir Alex also coined the phrase 'squeaky-bum time' and this is now in the *Oxford English Dictionary*.

OCH, CANADA

7

Canada only looks like it does today thanks to Glasgow-born Sir John Macdonald. The country's first prime minister, he served 19 years in the job. It was thanks to his national vision that a relatively small colony expanded to cover the northern half of North America. Macdonald also helped open up the west of the vast nation by building the world's longest railway, the Canadian Pacific, which was completed today in 1885. Of Canada's 22 prime ministers, an impressive 13 are of Scottish heritage.

RETIRING ON TOP

8

T. Macari from Rosyth stunned the world when he recaptured the world long jump record today in 2012. Earlier in the year the amazing athlete had leaped a world-beating 30cm, only to see his record beaten by rivals from around the world. Undaunted, the plucky Scot came out of retirement to mark up a mighty 48cm, once more taking the world record for our proud nation. If 48cm doesn't seem that impressive, you should know that T. Macari – 'Truffles' to his friends – is a guinea pig.

LETTERS AFTER HIS NAME

George Bruce is one of those unsung inventors who is better known abroad than here. After emigrating from Scotland to the United States, he did nothing less than revolutionise the printing industry. One of the most successful type designers of the nineteenth century, he was awarded the first-ever 'design patent', an industrial design milestone, for his fonts today in 1842. He also standardised type sizes and created many beautiful typefaces that are still popular.

AT VICTORIA FALLS, TURN LEFT

David Livingstone knew where he was today in 1871 – doing his missionary work near Lake Tanganyika. But the outside world hadn't heard from him in six years and thought him dead. So when Henry Stanley stumbled into a clearing and said, 'Dr Livingstone, I presume?' it really was remarkable. Livingstone had risen from poverty in Blantyre to become a heroic missionary, anti-slavery campaigner and explorer. He was the first European to see the Victoria Falls and the first to traverse Africa – though not the first to get lost there.

LEE-DING THE WAY IN RIFLE DESIGN

James Paris Lee was born in Hawick and immigrated to North America, where he made his name as a gun designer. His biggest innovation was the bolt system for the rifle that bears his name – the Lee-Enfield. Reliable and rugged, this was the British Army's standard rifle from its official adoption today in 1895 until 1957. To this day, the rifle is used by many armed forces around the world.

IKE LIKED IT

Next time you're tootling along the A719 south of Dunure, watch out for the Electric Brae. Stop your car on this section of road with the handbrake off and it will magically roll off uphill. It seems supernatural, but it's really an optical illusion – one of the world's few 'gravity hills'. General Eisenhower was given a flat in nearby Culzean Castle, today in 1945, as thanks for America's support during the Second World War, and when he visited he always used to bring his pals over to enjoy the Brae.

HE HAD A WHALE OF A TIME

Christian Salvesen was Norwegian, but he moved here in 1851 and established his company in Leith. It became the biggest whaling company in the world, at a time when it wasn't thought bad form to harpoon the poor devils. Salvesen also founded the settlement of Leith Harbour (named after his base in Scotland) on the island of South Georgia today in 1909. Happily, the firm got out of whaling in 1963 and instead became one of the world's biggest logistics corporations – the smart new word for shipping companies.

M^C^MOON MEN

US astronaut Alan Bean packed a piece of his kilt when he blasted off on the *Apollo 12* mission today in 1969. Proud of his Scottish heritage, he took the 14-inch-square section of MacBean tartan all the way to the moon's surface when he became the fourth man to step on it. Neil Armstrong, the first man on the moon, also had Scots ancestry and delighted the residents of Langholm when he accepted their invitation to become a freeman of the town in 1972.

KING OF CREATION

15

Alan McGee from East Kilbride was working for British Rail when he formed a wee indie record label and released a single by an old school pal's band today in 1984. The band was The Jesus and Mary Chain, who became an underground sensation. The pal was Bobby Gillespie, whose next band would be Primal Scream. McGee later added My Bloody Valentine and Teenage Fanclub to his roster, and by the time he signed Oasis, Creation Records was easily the most influential indie music label ever.

SPECIAL AIR STIRLING

16

The SAS is one of the world's most fearsome elite fighting forces, and that's not surprising, considering its founder. David Stirling was a Scottish laird, Commando officer and all-round nutcase: Montgomery called him 'mad, quite mad', and he was known to have personally strangled 41 men. Although his new unit (which first saw action today in 1941) would be ground-based, Stirling called it the 'Special Air Service' to deliberately misinform the enemy. They remained misinformed for about 3½ minutes before being comprehensively battered.

BIG ON BOOKS

Scotland has a proud literary heritage and no wonder – the Mitchell Library in Glasgow is the largest public reference library in Europe. Opened today in 1877, its beautiful building houses 1.2 million volumes and the world's largest Robert Burns collection. Its extensive and enticingly warm reading rooms are also rumoured to hold the world record for 'most tramps simultaneously asleep behind an upside-down newspaper'.

BOLDLY GOING WHERE NO WOMAN HAD GONE BEFORE...

Sophia Jex-Blake wanted to be a doctor. The only problem was that she was born in the middle of the nineteenth century, an era when men strictly ruled the medical roost. Sophia was turned down flat by Harvard and every single medical school in England. Finally, Edinburgh University took a bold leap and admitted her. Six other women soon joined her, creating the first group of female medical undergraduates at a British university. Today in 1870 they became the first women to sit a medicine examination. Sophia later established pioneering medical schools for women in London and Edinburgh.

FLUSHED WITH PRIDE

It's World Toilet Day, the perfect time to celebrate Alexander Cummings, the Edinburgh-born watch-maker who became the first person to patent a design of flush toilet. Cummings was a mathematician and mechanic as well as a watchmaker, but his best motion – sorry, notion – was his 1775 design of an 'S-trap', which used standing water to prevent the escape of foul air from the sewer and swirling water to clean the bowl. This basic idea is still in use today.

ELEMENTARY EDUCATION

Sherlock Holmes' powers of close observation and logical deduction were based on author Sir Arthur Conan Doyle's old Edinburgh University professor, Dr Joseph Bell. In his classes, Bell would often pick a stranger and, by observing him, deduce his occupation and recent activities. Sherlock Holmes first appeared in 'A Study in Scarlet', a story featured in *Beeton's Christmas Annual*, published today in 1887.

NORTHERN EXPOSURE

Hats (and everything else) off to Laird Michael Dudgeon, who today in 2003 opened one of the largest nudist beaches in Europe as a boost to local tourism. How successful this has been is unclear, as it is also the coldest nudist beach in the known universe, being at Crakaig in Sutherland, just 40 miles from John O'Groats. There is only one other official nudie beach in Scotland and no, sadly, it's not at the Butt of Lewis, nor the Cock of Arran.

REALLY RALLY FAST

Lanark-born Colin McRae was one of the most thrillingly gifted drivers of all time. He excelled on motorbikes in his early teens before burning up tracks behind a steering wheel. In 1991 and 1992 he was British Rally Champion. In the 1995 World Rally Championship he was 30 points off the lead with only 4 races to go, but somehow he managed to blast his Subaru Impreza 555 to victory. Today he became the first British person and the youngest driver ever to win the title, a record he still holds.

DOCTOR WHAE?

A Scotsman is responsible for more children hiding behind sofas than anyone else. Donald Wilson from Dunblane was head of Auntie's script department when BBC TV wanted a new family show. Wilson and his writers came up with *Doctor Who*, which was first broadcast tonight in 1963. The programme was originally intended to be educational, with the time-travelling Doctor introducing children to historical events. Kids, of course, much preferred being scared stiff by Cybermen.

SAINT WHAE?

It's easy to overlook St Kilda, as the archipelago is 40 miles further into the Atlantic than the most westerly of the Western Isles. But it is simply one of the most amazing places in the world. Its 1,400ft sea cliffs are the highest in the UK, its Soay sheep were the first breed domesticated in Europe and it has more seabirds than you can shake a puffin at. Officially recognised as awesome by UNESCO today in 1986, it is one of the few places on the planet that makes the grade for its natural and cultural treasures. Curiously, no one is sure where the name comes from – there has never been a saint called Kilda.

MUSICAL MILLIONS

Cambuslang-born Midge Ure was rehearsing with his band Ultravox for an episode of *The Tube* when host Paula Yates passed him the phone. On the line was her then husband, Bob Geldof, who was ranting about the Ethiopian famine and had some lyrics for a song. Midge worked up the music and today in 1984, Band Aid gathered in a London recording studio to sing 'Do They Know It's Christmas'. Ure and Geldof hoped it might raise £70,000; it became the biggest-selling single in UK chart history, shifting 3.5 million copies and raising millions of pounds.

THE COLOSSUS OF ROADS

If anyone paved the way for Britain's industrial development it was Thomas Telford. The son of a shepherd, he was born in Dumfriesshire and became an apprentice stonemason. But he made his name as a civil engineer, designing the Ellesmere Canal with its spectacular Pontcysyllte Aqueduct (opened today in 1805), which carries narrowboats more than 120ft above the valley floor. He also built the Menai Suspension Bridge, St Katharine Docks in London, the Göta Canal in Sweden, hundreds of bridges and thousands of miles of roads. It's thanks to Telford that the Highlands became in any way accessible, all of which makes you wonder why it was left to England to name a town after him.

LOOK INTO MY EYES...

James Braid from Kinross was a skilled surgeon who gave up correcting club feet to develop his own method of the new phenomenon of 'mesmerism'. Braid began lecturing on the subject today in 1841 and showed that hypnotism was physiological rather than some sort of clairvoyance. He coined the term 'hypnotism' and is considered to be the first genuine hypnotherapist.

THIS IDEA GETS UNDER YOUR SKIN

Fife-born doctor Alexander Wood was out and about when a bee alighted on his arm and very deliberately began to insert its sting in his flesh. At which point most sensible people would yell, 'Aiyah bampot!' and run round in circles. Wood, however, promptly went back to his lab and invented the hypodermic syringe. And, this being before the days of such things as research or medical trials, he simply tried his idea out by making the first-ever subcutaneous injection, when he administered morphia to a patient today in 1853.

THE WILLY WONKA OF TANNOCHSIDE

After paying £80 for premises in Uddingston, Thomas Tunnock had his baker's shop up and running by today in 1890. Tunnock's remained a humble bakers until the 1950s, when the company hit a spectacular purple snack patch, inventing Caramel Wafers, Snowballs, Caramel Logs and Teacakes in quick succession. Total world teatime domination followed swiftly. Nowadays there is a year's wait for a factory tour and Tunnocks Teacakes get squished before breaktime in school lunchboxes in 30 countries around the world.

ST ANDREW'S DAY

St Andrew is an odd choice of national saint, as he never went anywhere near Scotland in his lifetime. Born on the Sea of Galilee, he was crucified at Patras on an X-shaped cross (hence the design of the saltire) at his own request as he felt unworthy of a Jesus-style cross. He is also the patron saint of Greece, Romania, Russia, Ukraine and the US Army Rangers but not, curiously, golfers.

DECEMBER

ISLAND INSPIRATION

1

The Coral Island is a novel written by Scottish author R.M. Ballantyne about three boys shipwrecked on a South Pacific island. The book first went on sale today in 1857 and has never been out of print. Although not so famous nowadays, it was a hugely influential piece of literature, knocking the socks off a young Robert Louis Stevenson and inspiring his 1882 novel *Treasure Island*. It also directly led William Golding to pen his dystopian masterpiece *Lord of the Flies*.

WILD AND WONDERFUL WEATHER

Our wild winter weather might not seem like anything to be proud of, but one particularly feisty gale in 1850 did something wonderful. Locals in the Bay of Skaill on Orkney found the storm had stripped the earth from a large knoll to reveal perfectly preserved ancient houses. Now known as Skara Brae, it is Europe's most complete Neolithic village. Occupied from 3180–2500 BC, it is older than Stonehenge and the Great Pyramids, and was inscribed as a UNESCO World Heritage Site today in 1999.

DISNEY DISNAE LIKE BEING A MOUSE

By 1947, chain-smoker Walt Disney was becoming too hoarse to voice Mickey Mouse. So he handed squeaking duties to Jimmy MacDonald, head of his sound effects department and a Dundonian (if only for six months). Jimmy voiced Mickey for nearly 30 years from the short film *Mickey and the Seal*, released today in 1948, onwards. Jimmy's high-pitched pipes can also be heard playing Chip (of Chip'n'Dale) and the Dormouse in *Alice and Wonderland*.

DESPERATE DANDEE

The *Dandy*, which first appeared today in 1937, was one of the world's longest-running comics. It was published by Dundee-based firm D.C. Thomson, which is famous for a whole stable of comics including the *Beano*, *Commando* and the *Sunday Post*. It also ceased print production on this day in 2012, its 75th anniversary, giving in to modern times and becoming a purely online comic. Cripes!

NO SLAVES IN SCOTLAND

Joseph Knight was sold by a slave-trader in Jamaica to John Wedderburn of Ballendean, who made Knight part of his household staff in Scotland. Although Wedderburn treated him fairly well, Knight wanted to leave his employment, and took his master to court. The case went all the way to the Court of Session, where Lord Kames made the historic ruling today in 1778 that Scots law could in no way recognise slavery. Knight was a free man. This was 29 years before slave trading was abolished in the British Empire, and 66 years before Britain finally abolished slavery itself.

THE KNOWLEDGE BUSINESS

The *Encyclopaedia Britannica* has been the world's foremost book of knowledge for nearly 250 years. It was first published in Edinburgh, today in 1768, and was the idea of Colin Macfarquhar, a bookseller, and Andrew Bell, an engraver. They chose a twenty-eight-year-old scholar named William Smellie as their editor, paying him £200 to produce the 3-volume, 2,391-page first edition. He did it in three years, although he did admit to pinching large chunks from other writers, including Voltaire, Pope and Johnson.

A REVOLUTIONARY IDEA

John Dunlop was an Ayrshire-born vet who wondered if he could make his son's tricycle any smoother to ride. He promptly developed the first practical pneumatic tyre, which he patented today in 1888. The Dunlop tyre became revolutionary in the development of road transport. However, his patent was later declared invalid as it was discovered the concept had been invented back in 1846. Luckily for us, this was by another Scot, Robert Thomson (see 16 June).

THE GENIUS'S GENIUS

Who did Einstein think was a genius? James Clerk Maxwell, that's who, the Scottish scientist who published his first scientific paper at the age of fourteen and went on to formulate the Electromagnetic Field Theory (first presented today in 1864). His ideas laid the foundation for satellite communications, radio, mobile phones and radar. In his spare time Maxwell created the first true colour photograph in 1861 – of a tartan ribbon.

THINGS ARE LOOKING ROSEY

Ah, that great Scottish drink, the vodka and lime... No? Well, the first factory producing lime juice was set up by Lauchlan Rose on Commercial Street in Leith. And today in 1867 Rose patented his unique method of preserving fresh lime juice without alcohol. That same year the Merchant Shipping Act had required all ships to provide a daily lime ration to sailors to prevent scurvy. 'Rose's Lime Juice' became nearly ubiquitous, hence the US term 'limey' first for British sailors, then applied to all of us. It also makes a mean mojito!

BONG TO RIGHTS

Next time you're busted, play the boffin card. Sir Alexander Todd was a Scottish biochemist whose research on nucleic acids led to the solution of the genetic code, cleared the path for the discovery of DNA, and won him the Nobel Prize for Chemistry (today in 1957). He also worked on the alkaloids in hashish, and once naively imported 6lb of distilled cannabis resin from the Indian police; UK Customs found this stash but let it through on the condition that Todd sent them 25 copies of his research paper.

BRITANNIA LAYS UP IN LEITH

Launched in 1953 from John Brown's shipyard in Clydebank, the Royal Yacht *Britannia* steamed 1,087,623 nautical miles in her lifetime, helping to make HM the Queen the most travelled monarch the world has ever known. After 44 years spent visiting the world's most glamorous locations, *Britannia* was retired today in 1997 and took up residence in the regal atmosphere of Leith Docks. That's some comedown.

CLIMBING THE WALLS

'Hey, I know what, let's build the world's largest indoor climbing centre in that manky old quarry,' sounds like a pub idea destined to get no further than the back of a soggy beermat. But the three climbing pals who came up with it only went and pulled it off. After four years of construction and 250,000 tonnes of rubble shifted, they realised their vision at Ratho, today in 2004. Some of its awesome climbing walls are the height of a 10-storey building. Which you don't want to muck about on after an evening in the pub...

NEW LANARK, NEW LIFE

New Lanark was founded in 1786 by David Dale, who built cotton mills and housing that offered decent living standards to his workers. Dale and his son-in-law, Robert Owen, showed that industry didn't have to mistreat its employees to be profitable. Owen opened the first infants' school in Britain there in 1817, and New Lanark became a landmark of socialism and urban planning. Today in 2001, New Lanark was inscribed on UNESCO's list of World Heritage Sites.

THE CLOCKWORK ORANGE

While the origin of the Glasgow Subway's literary nickname is open to debate, we do know that the railway that opened today in 1896 is the third-oldest underground metro system in the world after the London Underground and the Budapest Metro. It has always been small: its circular lines are just 6.5 miles long and its 4ft track gauge makes for dinky trains. And while it may not be the world's first underground system, it is definitely the world's shoogliest.

AS EXOTIC AS THAILAND – OFFICIALLY

15

A lazy marketing exec in the Thai tourist industry couldn't be bothered going to take a photo of Kai Bae beach so he just found a nice shot on the internet. Unluckily for him, the shot he chose for his advert today in 2009 was actually of West Beach on Berneray, in the Hebrides. The ivory sands, turquoise waters and distant mountains do look beautiful, but the distinct lack of mangrove swamps and coconut trees should have given the game away.

YULETIDE CHEER FOR LEITH

You can thank (or blame) a printer in Leith, Charles Drummond, for the endless fun of writing out your Christmas cards. Tonight in 1841 Drummond placed a card in his Kirkgate shop window featuring a laughing, chubby-cheeked boy with the line: 'A gude New Year and mony o' them'. Within two years cards were all the rage as Victorians threw themselves into creating the modern concept of Christmas. Bah, humbug!

SHOP TILL IT DROPS

'Modernist masterpiece' is how Cumbernauld Shopping Centre was described when it opened in 1967. Indeed, it was the first indoor shopping mall in Britain and the world's first multi-level covered town centre. And in 1981 it was the setting for the uplifting movie *Gregory's Girl*. But in reality it was a concrete catastrophe that started falling down before it was even completed. Still, we can be proud that it achieved another first today in 2005 when it was voted the 'worst building in Britain'.

ODE TO A MOSQUITO

Before Ronald Ross, people thought malaria was transmitted by 'bad air' – hence the name. The son of the celebrated Scottish soldier Sir Campbell Ross, Ronald graduated in medicine in 1880 and spent the next two decades studying malaria in India. He was the first to demonstrate the complicated life cycle of the malarial parasite, including its presence in the mosquito's salivary glands. His landmark paper was published in the *British Medical Journal* today in 1897. He then pioneered an intensive programme of worldwide disease prevention, saving millions of lives. On top of all that, Ross's poetry was also pretty damned amazing too!

THE MORE THE MERRIER

You may have heard the principle that virtue provides 'the greatest happiness for the greatest numbers' – well, it was coined by Francis Hutcheson, who became professor of moral philosophy at Glasgow University today in 1729. Hutcheson practised what he preached, delivering brilliant and famously entertaining lectures that drew students from all over Britain, including Adam Smith. Mind you, they may also have come because Hutcheson was known to be happy to act as a banker to his students.

HAD BY A HAGGIS

A sheep's heart, liver and lungs minced with onion, oatmeal and spices all boiled up in the animal's stomach – haggis is one of those dishes that makes you wonder what the heck its inventor was thinking of. Still, it's so delicious it has its own poem: the 'Address to a Haggis' by Robert Burns, which was first published today in 1786. We can also be proud of the fact that 33 per cent of Americans have officially bought our wind-up that a haggis is a wee beastie with its legs longer on one side for manoeuvring on Scottish hillsides.

CHALLENGING SCIENCE

Little was known of the open ocean, or even how deep it really was, until Wyville Thomson, a botanist from Linlithgow, launched one of the greatest ventures in science today in 1872. Aboard the ship *Challenger*, Thomson led a three-year surveying voyage of 70,000 nautical miles. He catalogued 4,700 previously unknown species and established the modern discipline of oceanography. While he was about it, he fathomed out the deepest point in the ocean, now known as the Challenger Deep.

TALKING HISTORY

James Burnett, Lord Monboddo, was a renowned Scottish judge who also goes down in our proud history for his phenomenal work as the founder of historical linguistics. Today in 1773 he published *The Origin and Progress of Language*, a radical analysis of primitive and modern languages. Years before anyone else, Monboddo theorised that all human origin was from a single area of the earth. His language analysis was all the more amazing because he was as deaf as a door.

UNIDENTIFIED FLEEIN' OBJECTS

Since the first sighting there today in 1992, the wee town of Bonnybridge has become the UFO capital of the world. There are now 300 sightings a year and almost half the town's residents claim to have spotted a UFO. This has led to the area being dubbed the 'Falkirk Triangle'. The fact that it is very near indeed to the 'Buckfast Triangle' – the area south of Cumbernauld that accounts for a huge proportion of worldwide consumption of Buckie – is purely coincidental.

THE BARRAS IS BOUNCING

There are plenty of bigger music venues than the Barras, but none better. Fans and bands love its insane atmosphere and in polls of musicians it has been voted both the best music venue in the UK and the second best in the world. It opened in its current form tonight in 1960, and its legendary acoustics hark back to the day when it was a dancehall – the Barrowland Ballroom. If those audiences could hear an unamplified orchestra, today's can certainly hear Metallica. There wasn't as much snakebite flying around in those days, though.

STONE WITH A NEW DESTINY

The Stone of Scone was used as the coronation stone for Scottish kings until it was pinched by Edward I in 1296 and taken to Westminster Abbey. Thenceforth used for English coronations, it remained in London for six centuries until this day in 1950, when it was stolen by four students with nationalist sentiments and a fast car. They eventually returned it, but their point had been made and the stone now sits in Edinburgh Castle ... between coronations, of course.

CARRON'S CANNON

With it first blast furnace operational from today in 1760, the Carron Company foundry in Stirlingshire went on to forge history. It perfected the carronade, a powerful, short-range weapon that delivered a massive weight of shot compared to a similarly sized cannon. French foundries couldn't match it for 20 years, so carronades gave British warships a massive tactical advantage: HMS *Victory* used them to great effect at the Battle of Trafalgar. By 1814 the foundry was the largest ironworks in Europe, and it later produced pillar boxes and classic red telephone boxes.

PETER FLIES INTO LITERARY HISTORY

The immortal character of Peter Pan first appeared on stage today in 1904 in the play of the same name. This was later developed into a hugely popular novel by its author J.M. (James Matthew) Barrie, a weaver's son from Kirriemuir. Before his death he presented the rights to Peter Pan to Great Ormond Street Hospital, which benefits from them to this day. The story also popularised the name Wendy.

TEN-GALLON BUNNET

Bathgate doesn't look much like Dallas, even on a good day. But when Glasgow chemist James Young worked out how to distil paraffin from coal he built a processing plant at Whiteside (opened today in 1851). This was the world's first oil refinery, nine years before the first well was drilled in the US. By 1870 there were 97 oil companies in West Lothian and Scotland was the world's leading oil producer. Young became the 'Father of the Oil Industry' and his profits supported the African ventures of his friend, another Scot: David Livingstone.

SKIFFLE SUPREMO

Not many people today realise that one of the most influential musicians of all time was Anthony Donegan from Glasgow. Better known as Lonnie, he was 'King of Skiffle' in the 1950s with 24 successive Top 30 hits. Easily Britain's most successful and influential recording artist before the Beatles, he was rated by them as a major inspiration. Paul McCartney said, 'We all bought guitars to be in a skiffle group. He was the man.' Lonnie's first big hit, 'Rock Island Line', got teenagers rocking when it was released today in 1955.

HAMILTON-TON-TON-TON-TON-TON...

Hamilton Mausoleum is a very remarkable building. For a start, its designer, the eccentric 10th Duke of Hamilton, took up residence there today in 1858 inside an Egyptian sarcophagus. Today, however, it is a mausoleum without any dead bodies: all the deceased dukes that it once housed were moved out when the building began to subside in 1921. Best of all, though, it has the longest-lasting echo of any building in the world – an impressive 15 seconds.

HOGMANAY

If there's one thing Scotland truly excels at it's a New Year knees-up: no one else in the world takes the day after the day after the party off as well. And Burns' 'Auld Lang Syne' is the world's favoured theme song for tonight's festivities. Although scholars disagree on the exact origins of the word 'hogmanay', many insist it is derived from the Gaelic for 'help me up'. So fill your glass, and let's raise a toast – to another year of proud Scottishness! Sláinte!

ACKNOWLEDGEMENTS

To my father, Mark.
He's Scottish and I'm proud of him,
365 days a year.

I would like to send a massive 'Cheers, pal' to all these lovely and wonderful people:

Jonathan Perkins at Stripe Communications and all at AG Barr for IRN-BRU facts – and making IRN-BRU, of course; Deborah Smith and all at Pelamis Wave Power for information and helping to save the planet; Margaret Paterson and all at Tunnocks for information about the legendary Thomas Tunnock; Rob Smith at Howdens Pet Store in Coldstream for his help with George Wilson, sheep-dipper extraordinaire; Scot Nicol at D&G Wildlife for ideas, inspiration and cheap entry to Historic Scotland sites!

Yer all magic, y'are.

There's a lot of fantasy about what Scotland is,
and the shortbread tins and that sort of thing.

SEAN CONNERY